P.S. I MISS YOU

P.S. I MISS YOU

JEN PETRO-ROY

FEIWEL AND FRIENDS

NEW YORK

A Feiwel and Friends Book

An imprint of Macmillan Publishing Group, LLC

175 Fifth Avenue, New York, NY 10010

Our books may be purchased in bulk for promotional, educational, or business use. Please contact your local bookseller or the Macmillan Corporate and Premium Sales Department at (800) 221-7945 ext. 5442 or by e-mail at MacmillanSpecialMarkets@macmillan.com.

Library of Congress Control Number: 2017944817

ISBN 978-1-250-12348-0 (hardcover) / ISBN 978-1-250-12347-3 (ebook)

Book design by Liz Dresner and Carol Ly

Feiwel and Friends logo designed by Filomena Tuosto

First Edition, 2018

10 9 8 7 6 5 4 3 2 1

mackids.com

FOR BRIAN. IT WAS WORTH IT.

Dear Cilla,

It's been twenty-four hours since you left. (Okay, twenty-three and a half.) It feels longer, though.

You've been away before. Sleepovers at your friends' houses. A drama club field trip for three nights last spring. Even church sleepover camp when you were in middle school. I was seven then, and I remember going to the mailbox every single day to see if you'd sent me a postcard. You only sent one dinky card that whole time, though. It didn't even have a picture of your camp on it, either, just a random picture of a sunset, with MAINE in big pink letters on the front.

The back was just as boring. I'd wanted to hear all about your new friends, about the new songs you'd been learning, and who snored at night. Instead I got messy handwriting and a jelly stain:

Dear Evie,

Camp is fun. The food is gross. Except for the s'mores. I could eat those forever.

Love,
Your sister,
Cilla

You put a heart above the *i* in your name, like you did all through middle school. You thought it made you super cool.

I thought it *did* make you super cool.

I still have that postcard in my keepsake box in the back of my closet. It's on top of the wreath of fake flowers I wore on my head for First Communion, the cross necklace Grandma left me in her will (and that Mom and Dad say is too special to *ever* wear), and the blue ribbon Maggie and I won at the science fair last fall.

Even if your postcard was only four lousy sentences, I still kept it. Because it meant you were thinking of me, even if only a little bit. That's why *I'm* writing to you, too. I'll write letters, though, which are way better than postcards. (Even if they don't have cool pictures.)

Real letters. On stationery and everything.

(Okay, another reason I'm writing on paper is that Mom says Aunt Maureen doesn't have cell access *or* Internet access on her farm. You'd probably get e-mails if she didn't basically live in the olden days. It would be way better if you could get this right away and I didn't have to wait a whole *week* for your answer.)

At least I finally get to use the stationery Aunt Megan got me for my birthday last year. Even if I'm totally not a "yellow and pink roses" kind of person.

Some of these letters might be short and some might be long. I'll keep sending them, though, so you'll know all about what's going on while you're away.

It must be lonely there.

Maybe I can keep you company.

Write back soon.

Love,
Evie

P.S. I miss you.

Dear Cilla,

I've checked the mailbox the past two days, but I still haven't gotten a letter from you. I wasn't that surprised, though. Virginia's pretty far from Massachusetts. I wonder if the mailman (or mailwoman!) will even be *able* to find Aunt Maureen's farm. Remember that time two years ago when we drove to Disney World and stopped at the farm on the way to Florida? Dad's GPS broke somewhere in New York, then he missed the exit in Virginia. We had to buy an actual map at a gas station to find our way to Aunt Maureen's.

While Dad was trying to read the map (and Mom teased him for being "directionally impaired"), we had lunch in the parking lot of that gross gas station on a picnic table covered with sticky grape juice. Or something else sticky that I don't want to think about. You ate those weird cheese and crackers where you spread the orange cheese with a little red plastic stick, and I had a stick of beef jerky because you dared me to. It was so salty that I needed *two* bottles of water to get the taste out of my mouth. I was so glad I'd convinced Mom to get me a bag of M&M's, too!

Dad finally navigated his way to Aunt Maureen's an hour later, after driving on about seven hundred narrow dirt roads and passing about two hundred cows. A few pigs, too. But when we got to the farm, there were no cows. No pigs, either. Not even a chicken. Aunt Maureen's place looked nothing like a farm. Yeah, she had the old red barn and the stables, but they were empty. There were no animals at all, just old Aunt Maureen (*Great*-Aunt Maureen, actually), an old dog named Buster, and an old house filled with yarn and knitting needles. (Those were probably old, too.)

Mom told us later that it *had been* a farm, until Great-Uncle Elliot died. That's when Aunt Maureen sold all the animals and basically turned into a shut-in. The place smelled like old lady, baked beans, and raisin toast.

Now you have to stay there until September. Three whole months of old lady, baked beans, and raisin toast. Knitting, too. Lots and lots of knitting.

And no Internet. I know *I* couldn't deal.

But that doesn't matter to Mom and Dad. They probably think it's a "fitting punishment" for what you did. Which, yeah, was pretty bad. I think. Honestly, I'm not sure if what you did was a sin anymore. I don't like to think of you as a sinner. You're my sister.

You're Cilla, who braids my hair every Friday before school.

Cilla, who didn't care that I stuck out my tongue and gagged when she told me about her first kiss with Alex.

Cilla, who steals all the cookie dough from the cookie dough ice cream and leaves me with just the boring vanilla.

Maybe you did something bad, but that doesn't mean I can't still write to you.

Even if Mom and Dad aren't.

Love,

Evie

P.S. I miss you.

Dear Cilla,

I'm not used to writing letters. Well, besides the thank-you notes Mom still makes me write to Grandma and Grandpa after my birthday and Christmas. Do you remember the year you refused to write thank-yous because you thought you'd thanked everyone enough in person? I thought Dad was going to throw your brand-new keyboard across the room. He didn't, though. He lectured you about respecting your elders and then let me play with the keyboard until your grounding was over, which was kind of awesome. I didn't want you to get un-grounded.

I'm ready for this punishment to be over, though.

Are you getting any of these letters? This is my third one and you still haven't written back. Are you ignoring me? Are my letters getting lost? That can happen. Maybe there's something wrong with the postal box by the school. My letters might be getting stuck somewhere the mailman can't reach them. There could be a mail thief on the loose!

Or not.

Maybe you just don't care anymore. You're so excited to be away from your mistakes that your boring little sister doesn't matter anymore.

I get why you agreed to stay with Aunt Maureen. Mom and Dad were embarrassed and you were embarrassed. You didn't want anyone to see your stomach. But I still don't understand why you agreed to go away to school *after* you have the baby. (Especially to an all-girls' Catholic school. An all-girls' Catholic *boarding* school. That sounds like the worst place in the world to run away to.)

You don't have to stay away once you have the baby. Things can go back to normal then. Maybe they can even go back to normal with Alex.

That's part of the reason I'm going to keep writing to you. Because I need to convince you to come home. I need to show you that things are going to be okay and you don't have to be ashamed anymore.

I need to tell you that I love you. And that even if they don't act like it, Mom and Dad do, too.

Love,
Evie

P.S. I still miss you.

Dear Cilla,

Today the town pool was closed. Something about chlorine issues. When Katie and Maggie and I got there at nine, the water looked green. Not leprechaun green or grass green, but more like limeade green. Limeade green with a tint of yellow, which made me think that some little kids had probably peed in there.

So even if there hadn't been a big CLOSED sign on the fence, there was no way we were putting a toe in that water. (Especially Katie, who'd painted her toes sparkly purple. She was ridiculously proud of them and kept looking at her toes as we walked to the pool. She almost walked into a STOP sign. Maggie and I laughed so hard that we lost our balance and almost fell into the sign, too.)

We decided to go to the park instead. I haven't been there in years. Remember how Mom and Dad always used to take us there after church when the weather was nice? First we'd have Mass, then we'd go to the doughnut social in the church hall. And then if we were *really* well behaved (which basically meant that you didn't sing at the top of your lungs and I didn't whine about how I was hungry the whole time), Mom and Dad would let us go to the park after.

You'd bring your tennis racket and hit the ball with Dad (until he convinced you to stop and throw a Frisbee around instead) and I'd go on the playground while Mom sat on the bench and watched me.

Then you'd get sick of Dad and we'd go down the twin slides at the same time, over and over again. You always reached the bottom first.

You always did everything first.

At least Mom and Dad never brought us to the park on the really hot days. That was today. It was ninety degrees by breakfast. The weather guy on TV called it a "scorcher" and said you could fry an egg on the sidewalk. Which, yeah, maybe you *could* do, but who would seriously want to eat that egg? Mmmm, I just love gravel omelets.

The pool would have been way better, but at least we put our blanket in the shade. Katie ran home (and came back covered in sweat) to get one. She also brought a cooler full of waters, watermelon, chocolate brownies, and Jolly Ranchers (which started to melt in about five seconds). Then Katie and Maggie stripped down to their bathing suits and started talking about Joey Witter, who was playing catch with Vivek Patel on the other side of the park.

They've decided that Joey is their newest crush and I've been pretending to agree with them, even though he's always mean to me. He made fun of me all last year because I got 100% on every spelling quiz. I know you said that means he likes me, but I think you're wrong. I think he's just mean. He talks to the lunch ladies more than he talks to me.

Swooning about Joey was really boring. Boring and hot. But even though I was sweating, I still wanted to go on the playground. It was in the sun, but there were still kids all over it, screeching and sliding and throwing sand. I didn't say anything to Maggie and Katie, though, because we're in seventh grade now. (Okay, almost in seventh grade.) We're too old for the playground.

That's what I'm supposed to think. But I really wanted to go on the tire swing, even though it was so hot, it would probably burn lines into my butt.

When I looked over, there was another girl on the tire swing already—and she looked around our age! She had dark skin and dark curly hair pulled back in a bright green headband. She was swinging slowly, and since she was the only one on the swing, it was tilting to one side. She grabbed on to a chain with one hand and held a book in the other.

Then Maggie poked me in the shoulder and asked me something about the Fourth of July celebration next week. I didn't really hear what she said, because I was too busy trying to see what the girl was reading. Even though seeing the title from our blanket would be pretty much impossible, since the tire swing was all the way across the park.

So Maggie poked me again. Then Katie poked me, too, which totally tickled. Which meant we *of course* ended up in a tickle fight like we were six years old.

When I looked up again, the girl was gone.

I don't know why I remembered all that—maybe because

it made me remember *us* on the playground, before everything changed. Maybe because it made me want to go back there.

Maybe because I was a little jealous of that girl, how she looked like she had nothing to worry about at all.

I bet *she* never had a sister get sent away.

Love,
Evie

P.S. I miss you.

Dear Cilla,

Okay, I know that technically Mom and Dad didn't send you away. They're not that cruel. They don't spank us or rap us on the knuckles with rulers or wash our mouths out with soap, all of that stuff you read about in old-fashioned books. (They don't even make us pray for hours every night. Just ten minutes. I can handle that.)

They didn't even pack your suitcase for you. You did that yourself, while I sat on the end of your bed and watched. First sweatpants. Then T-shirts. Then underwear, socks, and bras. Some regular clothes, but mostly the secondhand maternity stuff you bought at Goodwill. Your room got emptier with each thing you added to the suitcase.

I got emptier.

But even if they didn't pack the suitcase, they *did* make you get to the point where you *wanted* to pack your suitcase. They made you feel so awful and ashamed that you wanted to leave. They made you feel like your life was over.

When I first found out about the pregnancy, you were different. You seemed happy. Nervous—yes. Freaked out—totally. But you kept saying how much you loved Alex. You kept saying how much you wanted to make it work.

I was at Katie's house after school the day I found out. We finished our homework and watched TV for a while.

Mrs. Foley asked me if I wanted to stay for dinner. Mr. Foley and Ben were at baseball practice and there was a huge pot of chicken soup on the stove.

"My family hates leftovers," Mrs. Foley said. She practically pushed me toward the phone. "It'll go to waste if you don't stay." It smelled delicious, so I called home. No one answered, which was weird, since you'd stayed home sick that day. I remembered that you tried to convince Mom to let you go to school since you had musical rehearsal, but she saw you throwing up and didn't let you.

Looking back, I don't know why I didn't figure it out earlier. You were throwing up almost every morning, and it's pretty impossible not to notice *that*, even though you always closed the door and turned on the fan. Barf stinks, no matter how much you try to hide it. I never thought you were pregnant, though. I thought you just had a stomach bug. Why would you be pregnant? We were supposed to wait until we got married to have kids. And that wouldn't be for years and years.

(You were pregnant, though. And I found out the worst way possible. By walking in on a fight. The first of many, many fights.)

I tried to call again. Still no answer. So I went home. I took a plastic container full of soup with me, too, some for me and some for you. I don't know what happened to that soup. I put it down somewhere during all the yelling and forgot about it.

I told Mrs. Foley that Mom would be okay if I walked

home alone. It was still light out, and I could see our porch through the woods. I could hear the yelling as I got closer. The windows were open.

"I didn't raise you like this!" That was Dad's voice, low and gravelly.

"Do you know what this is going to look like?" Mom's voice, high and shrill like a bird's. "Do you know how this will change your life?"

I didn't know what they were talking about, but I knew I didn't want to go inside. I hovered outside the porch door. It started to rain. I would have rather been soaking wet than inside, though. I felt so bad for you, especially since you'd been barfing all morning.

"I love him." That was you. Do you remember saying that? It made you seem so grown-up. You loved someone. You, Priscilla Anne Morgan, loved someone. It made you seem older than sixteen and made me feel way younger than eleven.

"You do not love him. You're sixteen years old." The rain started coming down harder. I couldn't see Dad's face, but I imagined his eyes bulging out and his cheeks turning bright red.

I didn't know what was going on. Mom and Dad loved Alex. Mom and Dad loved you. Why were they so mad? Then the phone rang.

"Jennifer? What? Evelyn left? No, she hasn't come home yet." I'd forgotten how overprotective Mrs. Foley is, even with me. There wasn't enough time to hide, either. Not that diving under a deck chair would do anything. Mom turned around and crooked a finger at me. "Never mind, she's here. Thanks for calling." She pulled open the door and yanked me inside. Her fingertips dug into my arm.

"What's going on?" I remember looking from Mom to Dad to you and back again. No one said anything. That's when I started to feel like *I* was going to throw up. Something was really wrong. I'd never seen our parents so angry.

"Priscilla," said Mom with a grimace, "apparently loves Alex."

Mom said this like it was a bad thing. Like it was a big news flash. It wasn't to me, though. I knew you loved Alex. You'd been telling me that for months. And I liked Alex. I liked how happy he made you.

"I *do* love Alex," you said.

"What's the big deal?" I asked.

"Alex is her baby's father." Mom pointed at your stomach. Dad sank down onto the couch.

I didn't know what to say. You weren't big, like the pregnant ladies I see on TV or at the mall. You were wearing a baggy T-shirt and sweatpants. But your face was pale and I could tell Mom was telling the truth.

It didn't make sense, though. You aren't the kind of girl who gets pregnant. Bad girls get pregnant, girls who have . . . you know.

I never thought of you as a bad girl. And you kept saying that you didn't do anything wrong. That things would be okay.

That you and Alex wanted to get married.

(That, as I'm sure you remember, is when Dad's face turned the shade of the eggplants Mom grows in our vegetable garden.)

You kept saying stuff like that for a few weeks, until you had that big fight with Alex. Until Mom and Dad finally wore you down.

Then it was perfectly fine to go to Aunt Maureen's for the summer.

It was perfectly fine to make a plan to go away to school in the fall.

It was perfectly fine to leave without saying good-bye.

Love,
Evie

P.S. Even if you did all that stuff, I *do* miss you. And *I'm* not ashamed of you.

Dear Cilla,

Mom and Dad still make me go to church, even though I'm mad at God. I'm mad that He let you get pregnant and I'm mad that He didn't listen to me when I prayed for you to change your mind and stay home to have the baby.

When I told Mom and Dad that, they told me that my feelings were *why* it was so important to go to church. Because I need to spend time with God to hear His answer.

I don't want to spend time with God, though. I want to spend time with you.

You're my sister. God's just the big guy in the sky who let Mom and Dad push you away. He's the one who made them feel ashamed of you.

Father O'Malley always says that everything happens because it's part of God's plan and that He'll give us the strength to get through anything as long as we turn to Him, but God had a really bad plan this time.

I've been praying pretty hard, too, and I still don't feel strong.

Love,
Evie

P.S. I miss you.

Dear Cilla,

This morning was the Fourth of July parade. Katie and Maggie and I got there extra early to get good seats by the side of the road. Not that it mattered, since everyone put out their seats a week ago. You always used to think that was funny, how everyone in our town stuck their lawn chairs out way before parade day and how they didn't strap them down or lock them up, either.

It's just this sea of Adirondack chairs and folding chairs and those low canvas ones, all the way from the Dunkin' Donuts at the rotary to the Dunkin' Donuts in the center, where the parade ends.

No one ever takes them, either. There's never an article in the paper talking about the local chair thief. Mom never hears rumors at church about our neighbors having nowhere to watch the parade, after all. People know the rules. They're honest.

I remember you were always surprised by this, like you expected the chairs to disappear overnight, stolen by some daring bandit.

I never thought it was weird, though. Maybe because "Thou shalt not steal" is a commandment. Maybe because I'd never think of stealing a chair, so I couldn't imagine anyone else doing it.

You could, though. You always saw the world a little differently. Like you lived in this weird cloudy area between real life and church life, real life and *Mom and Dad* life. Maybe it was those clouds that got you in trouble.

Or maybe you were the only one who could see the storm coming.

Love,
Evie

P.S. I miss you.

Dear Cilla,

I totally forgot to tell you about the parade yesterday. I started thinking about clouds and you and got all sad. The parade was fun. I guess. It was the same as every year. Kids cried when the fire engines and police cars went by, and then started rushing the street when the creepy-looking clown rode by on his little bike and threw out candy. They had Spider-Man and Hermione throwing candy.

Katie's little brother pretended to be all cool about it, but I could tell he was totally freaking out. He has Spider-Man sheets and Spider-Man wallpaper and was Spider-Man for Halloween last year. I was more excited about Hermione, even though the person in the costume looked about thirty years old.

It started to rain halfway through, but it was only a drizzle so we still went to the carnival in the center. Pretty much everyone from school was there, except Miri Doherty, who always goes to Cape Cod for the summer. She has a house there and won't shut up about how awesome it is.

"It's almost on the water." Miri always tells us this with an annoying smirk on her face, like she knows she's better than everyone else. Which she's totally not. "All I have to do is walk down a little path and I'm at the beach. It has five bedrooms, too. Mine's the biggest."

Mom and Dad say material stuff like that doesn't matter, but sometimes I think they're wrong. Because it would be pretty great to have a house on the beach. Maybe then Mom and Dad would let you stay there instead of in Nowheresville, Virginia. Then I could visit you.

Everyone else besides Miri was there, though. Joey and Vivek came right from their baseball game and were still in their maroon-and-white uniforms. Joey offered me a bite of his cotton candy, but I said no. Cotton candy is gross. I know you don't agree, but it totally is. (And you're not here, so you can't argue back. Ha!)

Ms. Simon from school was in the dunk tank. Not like it mattered, because she'd been up there so long that she was already wet from the rain. Katie and Maggie bought a few tickets. I think they were still mad at Ms. Simon for all those spelling tests she gave last year. They didn't dunk her, though. Neither did Joey.

Vivek did, but only once. He bought three balls, too.

Ms. Simon is really young and funny, so she started making faces at the boys, which made them super upset. They started pretending they were missing on purpose. No one believed them, though. I thought Joey was going to throw a tantrum.

The boys were all arguing about whether the game was rigged when we heard a splash behind us. Then Ms. Simon popped up out of the water.

"Nice! You got it on the first try!" she cheered. Everyone

around us started clapping for whoever threw the ball. When I looked to see who it was, I saw the girl from the playground! You know, the one who was on the tire swing reading a book. Today she didn't have a book, but I still couldn't see her face. She was looking down at the ground as everyone cheered for her.

I waited until she finally looked up. A few of the curls around her face were dyed pink, which both surprised me and made me totally jealous. I've never known anyone with dyed hair before.

(Well, except for Mom, who dyes her gray hairs. I bet all her mom friends do that, too.)

I've never known anyone my age who dyed their hair, though. I wonder if Father O'Malley will let her in church like that.

Even if her hair *was* dyed, though, she looked nice. She was wearing a bright green skirt and this cool tank top with pink and green polka dots. Pink polka-dot sneakers, too!

I totally want polka-dot sneakers now.

Joey and Vivek kept saying stuff about "beginner's luck" and how she must have cheated, so the girl started to walk away. I didn't blame her, either. Joey can be really mean. (Which is another reason why I could never like him.)

I ran toward her. I almost tripped over a crack in the sidewalk, and to catch my balance, I grabbed on to her arm. She almost fell over, which meant that I almost fell onto her. On the wet sidewalk covered with drips of mustard and cheesy nacho crumbs. She gave me a dirty look, but I must have looked as horrified as I felt, because she started smiling. Then she pretended to be falling again.

I smiled, too. It felt like I'd been teetering over the edge of a cliff and someone had pulled me back. Where the cliff was being this girl's mortal enemy.

Or something like that.

Anyway, she smiled again. She had braces, and the elastics were pink, the same as her hair. It was the first time I'd seen someone make braces look cool. Then she turned around and walked away. I didn't see her the rest of the day, even though we stayed at the carnival until after lunch. I wonder if she's new. We haven't had a new girl in school in two years, ever since Zoe Holt showed up and became Miri's BFF.

After lunch, I won the ring toss game three times in a row, but the guy behind the booth only gave me a prize once. Which is totally unfair and totally against what it said on the sign. I still got a stuffed animal, though. It was a koala bear, your favorite.

I put it on your bed, next to Cuddly the koala. You can sleep with both of them when you get home if you want, even though I'm sure you don't sleep with stuffed animals anymore. It makes me feel good to think they're both waiting for you, though.

Because I know that you'll come home. Even if Mom and Dad say you're going to Catholic school right after you have the baby. Even if it was your idea to go to Catholic school, I know you'll change your mind. You'll realize that you belong here.

You have to.

Love,

Evie

P.S. Because I miss you.

Dear Cilla,

It's been almost a month now and you still haven't written back. Are you mad at me? Did I not do enough to convince Mom and Dad that you should keep the baby?

(You know, when you still *wanted* to keep the baby.)

I'm sorry if I let you down. I was just so surprised. Scared and confused, too. I didn't know what to say to you. You were Cilla, but all of a sudden you were this other person, too. This other person who'd done stuff I could never even dream of. Who'd broken commandments and actually *sinned*.

Plus, you guys were yelling all the time. I spent half of every weekend in my room with my earbuds in. (And I could *still* hear Mom and Dad screaming about "purity" and "honor" and your "reputation.")

You spent the *other* half of every weekend in your room. (And weeknights with Alex.)

I know you think I don't know about that, but I'm not stupid. I'm not a little kid, either. I saw his car parked at the end of the street. I heard you through the wall when you guys were on the phone.

That's another reason why I didn't defend you. Because I was mad at you. I was mad at you for ignoring me for *him*. I was mad at you for fighting with Mom and Dad so much that they turned into different people.

They started yelling at me about stuff, too. Silly stuff, like forgetting to unload the dishwasher and not wiping my feet on the mat. They treated me like *I* got pregnant in high school, too. Like getting the floor messy was the same as having . . . you know.

It's the eleventh commandment, you know: "Thou shalt not track dirt."

So that's why I wasn't on your side. When you said that you could figure out how to be a Broadway actress and still have a baby. When you were yelling about love and how you didn't care what people thought of you. Because right then, I *did* care what people thought. Because you were ruining my life.

I know I can't change what I did now, but I want you to know I'm sorry. I'm so sorry. I keep picturing you at Aunt Maureen's, knitting a sweater and eating stinky baked beans. Instead of here, living your life. Maybe you could play Mary in some nativity play somewhere. Or another pregnant character. I'm sure they're out there.

That's why I want you to write back. We need to talk about how you *need* to come home after you have the baby. How your life is still here. You don't need Catholic school. You don't have to be ashamed. You've learned your lesson and won't sin again.

Right?

Love,
Evie

P.S. I miss you.

Dear Cilla,

You woke me up the night everything changed. I'd slept over at Maggie's the night before and had gotten something like three hours of sleep, so I'd gone to bed early. It was probably only ten o'clock when I heard the yelling, but it felt like the middle of the night. It was dark and cloudy and there were no stars in the sky.

I still remember how there were no stars. No brilliance, no light, nothing twinkling at all.

I heard Dad first, with that big, booming voice he uses when he's really, really mad. Like when Hunter McCoy next door drove his truck over our lawn a week after he'd gotten his license. Or when I threw a baseball inside the house and broke the TV.

Dad gets mad when things break. And maybe to him, you broke something. Our family. His image of you. Your future.

I knew why he was yelling the second I heard him. You guys had been yelling for months. Him telling you not to complain about your morning sickness because getting pregnant was "your choice." Mom crying about how you'd never get a good job if this got out. You sobbing about how you still loved Alex, then sobbing about how they made him break up with you.

So when Dad yelled that you were an embarrassment, I

thought it would be the same old thing. It'd last fifteen minutes and then you'd all go in different directions. To be continued next time.

You guys *never* resolved anything. They yelled about how you shouldn't tell anyone you were pregnant. You yelled about how they weren't the only ones hurting. You all blamed everyone else and the conversation went round and round and round.

It was like one of those pictures of a snake eating its own tail. Or that optical illusion with the staircases that never stop going upward. No one ever apologized and the yelling never stopped. I'd started to expect that it would go on like that until the baby popped out of you. Then we'd all stare at it with confused expressions on all our faces: "Now what?"

It was different that night, though. When Mom (for the zillionth time) talked about how embarrassed she'd be at church if anyone knew, there was a big crash from downstairs. I don't know if you threw something or knocked something over. I don't know if it was God's way of telling me something important was about to happen.

First there was a bang. Then there was you: "If you're so embarrassed, why don't I just go away? So no one can *ever* see me like this."

I'd crept to the top of the stairs by this point. I was hugging the wall, partially for privacy and partially because I needed something to hold me up. Because you sounded like you meant it.

I expected Mom and Dad to say something like, "Oh,

honey, don't say things like that. We'll be mad at you for a while, but then things will get better."

You know, exactly what I wanted to hear.

They didn't say that, though.

Mom said that she *was* ashamed of you, because you'd done something shameful.

Dad said that's why they weren't telling anyone.

You said you couldn't live in a house like this anymore and you *were* going to leave.

Dad said, "Fine, you do that!"

Mom said, "Fine! I'll call Aunt Maureen. You can stay with her."

I was around the corner now, peeking through the banister like a little kid checking to see what Santa had left for her under the tree. Your eyes were open wide. You looked the way I feel when I'm at the end of the diving board with a long line behind me. When I don't want to jump off but I know I can't go back.

"Fine," you said. "I'll go. And maybe I won't come back after that." You said it softly, slowly, like you were waiting for them to interrupt you, like you were dipping one toe into the ocean to test the water.

The water was cold, though. Ice cold.

"You do that." Mom's voice was ice cold, too. "If you feel so strongly about leaving us, then we'll find you a school for you to go to after. One that's far, far away from here."

"So you don't have to deal with us and our silly morals," Dad added.

"Fine."

"Fine."

"Fine."

It wasn't fine at all. But after that, no one backed down. Even when you told me afterward that you shouldn't have said anything, that you *want* to come home after you have the baby.

I agree with you. It *was* a mistake.

Please come home.

Love,
Evie

P.S. I miss you.

Dear Cilla,

Mom and Dad want me to forget about you. They never say your name. They took your school pictures off the wall. Now all I see are a bunch of squares of darker wallpaper. Mom covered one of the squares with a painting of a maple tree. It's really ugly.

Sometimes it seems like the last few months were just a dream. Or a plot on some TV show I saw late one night. The episode where someone's sister gets pregnant and throws up all the time and grows out of her clothes and eats all the grapes and chocolate chip cookies in the house. The episode where someone's sister fights with her parents *all* the time.

Then someone changed the channel and it all went away. I still remember bits and pieces of the plot, but everything's fuzzy.

Two days after the big blowup, you were gone. We were supposed to go to the mall that morning. You were supposed to leave in the afternoon.

Instead, I woke up to Dad sitting at the kitchen table alone. You and Mom had left before the sun came up. You hadn't said good-bye.

When Mom came home I didn't say anything.

Neither did they.

We haven't since.

Maybe that's why I keep writing to you. Even if they're just words on a page, they're still words.

It makes the quiet a little less quiet.

Love,
Evie

P.S. I miss you.

Dear Cilla,

I looked for that girl in church today. Which was really awkward, since Mom and Dad still refuse to sit anywhere but the second row and I kept having to twist around to see the rest of the congregation.

I thought I might be able to convince them to change seats just this one time, but they were totally stubborn. As usual.

Dad had a cold and was sneezing every two minutes, so I told them they should stand in the back, that Dad was a health risk to the entire town. I said it in a super-dramatic voice: "TO THE *ENTIRE* TOWN!" (Picture me with my mouth and eyes wide open.)

It didn't change their minds even the teensiest bit, though. Dad blew his nose, and then they waltzed down the aisle to our usual seats. Second row, right side of the church, halfway down the pew, between Mr. and Mrs. Mara and the triplets of doom and Mr. MacKinnon's wheezy laugh. The spot might as well have our names written on the wood in permanent marker.

I'm glad it doesn't, though. Because then I'd have a big empty "Cilla" spot next to me, a reminder that you're not here because you don't belong here anymore.

Or at least that's what Mom and Dad think. I still don't think God would kick you out of church for having a baby.

And if He wouldn't, then why should Mom and Dad? When I asked them that, they said that they didn't kick you out, you'd just decided to "relocate" until the baby was born and you weren't so "conspicuous."

Which basically means that they're embarrassed by you. Which is gross.

I'm really disappointed in them. Which is weird. It makes me feel all grown-up, like I should send them to their room.

You know what else was disappointing? The girl wasn't in church. I looked back so many times that Mom yelled at me (well, she *whisper*-yelled) to stop. But then when it was Communion time, I watched everyone go down the aisle. I guess that's one good thing about sitting in the front.

I still didn't see her. Maybe she's not new. Maybe she was visiting for the summer. Or she's Baptist or Jewish.

Not that that's a bad thing. It'd just be cooler if she belonged to our church.

Love,
Evie

P.S. I miss you.

Dear Cilla,

Why did you have to get pregnant? Didn't you get the same lecture I did? Mom sat me down last year to talk about my "holy body" and how sex was a gift I should only give to my husband. She told me about Hell and sinning and how we go to church to learn how to live in God's image. Didn't she tell you that? Why didn't you listen?

If you had listened, things would be normal now. We'd be watching Pixar movies on the couch until Mom shouted at us that we were "wasting the day!" We'd be at the pool and I'd be avoiding looking at you and Alex kissing. We'd be eating way too many of Mom's famous peanut butter cookies.

Instead, you're doing whatever chores you do at a fake farm. And I'm looking for ghost girls at church while my hand falls off from writing so many letters.

Your sister,
Evie

P.S. I'm so mad at you today.

Dear Cilla,

It's Vacation Bible School week! Woo-hoo!

Can you tell I'm being sarcastic? Or did you really picture me jumping up and down on my bed and throwing confetti and glitter into the air?

Okay, maybe I might have done that when I was little. But that's because Vacation Bible School was *cool* when we were little. When we got to sit in a circle and sing church songs at the top of our lungs. When we got to make lists of why Jesus loves us and got a Skittle for every reason. When we had water balloon fights in the church parking lot and waited in line for the ice cream truck.

That was fun. I was a kid then, though. All my friends were there, too. Now I'm the only one left. I'm not even a camper anymore, either. I've aged out, but Mom and Dad are still making me help out as a counselor.

An "assistant" counselor. Which I'm not sure is an actual thing, since I'm going to be the only assistant there. I think it's just a way for Mom and Dad to make sure I'm being supervised. Because they've been extra clingy lately. Mom follows me around the house and Dad keeps asking me who I'm hanging out with.

Like just because you got pregnant I'm going to join a gang and start swearing.

I told Mom and Dad that I didn't need camp, that there was a middle ground between a week of extra church and becoming a Satan-worshipper. Something like, oh, hanging out with my friends? Being a *normal* kid?

Do you know what Dad said then? He said that I'm at a vulnerable age and it's a good idea to spend as much time with church people as possible. (And by "church people" he means other grown-ups and sticky six-year-olds.)

Like their prayers are going to stop me from turning into you.

I like you, though. I love you. I wouldn't mind being you at all.

(I almost crossed that out because it's super embarrassing, but I decided to leave it in. Just don't mention it when—yes, *when*—you come home in a few weeks. I'll turn so red it'll look like I got a sunburn.)

Okay, so maybe that will be the good part about Vacation Bible School. The sun. I'll get to spend time outside.

I'm *really* reaching here.

Love,
Evie

P.S. Vacation Bible School would be way better if you were there with me.

P.P.S. Because I miss you!

Dear Cilla,

It rained *all* week.

I didn't see the sun once.

We didn't even get to do water balloons.

I made about five thousand peanut butter and jelly sandwiches.

I left church every day smelling like the popcorn machine.

A little boy spilled green paint all over my favorite pink shorts and when I yelled at him, Father O'Malley told me I wasn't setting a good Catholic example.

Mom and Dad told me I couldn't be an assistant again next year.

Darn.

Love,
Evie

P.S. I miss you.

Dear Cilla,

I saw your friend Emma this morning. I was riding my bike and she was walking Bruno. I hate Bruno. Every time he sees me he barks like crazy and bares his teeth. His *sharp* teeth. Emma always says that's how he expresses affection, but I don't buy it. I don't bite people to show my love. Neither should dogs.

Emma asked about you. She said she misses you. She asked when you were coming home. She asked about the baby.

Which made me gasp. Literally gasp, like I was on one of those cheesy shows you used to watch, where there was always a BIG REVEAL! I couldn't help it, though. I didn't know you had told any of your friends about the baby.

But it's not like Mom and Dad muzzled you. Or caged you up before you started to show. You still went to school. You still hung out with your friends. Of course you told some of them. Emma assured me she'd kept your secret, though, so I guess you must not have told too many people. Then she asked me when you were coming home.

She didn't know about Catholic school! (Maybe I should use its fancy-pants name: Saint Augustine's School for Girls. Oooh la la!) She said you hadn't told her anything about staying away, only about leaving to have the baby. She looked really upset.

That made me feel a little bit better and a little bit worse.
Because at least I'm not the only one you're abandoning.

But that still doesn't mean anything is going to change.

You're still not here.

And I am.

Love,

Evie

P.S. I miss you.

Dear Cilla,

School starts next week. I have Mr. Barrett for homeroom. Mom said you had the other teacher, Mrs. Hazel, when you were in seventh grade. I'm glad I don't have her. Once Mom reminded me, I remembered how you'd complain all the time about how mean she was. Mr. Barrett is supposed to be the "nice" teacher. I hope that's true.

You haven't written back *still*. I've been writing to you for more than two months now. This is why e-mail is way easier. Or the phone (even though I know you don't like to talk on the phone). I could call you, you could pick up, and I'd tell you that you don't have to be ashamed anymore.

That even if Mom and Dad *convinced* you that you're a bad person, you're really not. That your future isn't ruined because you got pregnant.

I'll help you make it good. Or I'll try.

Your due date is really soon—we don't have much time left. I'm sure there will be paperwork to do and refunds to get from Saint Augustine's.

Ugh. *Saint Augustine's*. It sounds so proper. When I went on the website, everyone was wearing uniforms. The girls had on these heavy blue-and-gold plaid skirts. They wore collared white shirts, too, the kind Grandma calls "blouses." The teachers all wore those pants Grandpa calls "slacks."

Adults are weird.

We need to save you from the Land of Blouses and Slacks! We need to return you to the Kingdom of Jeans and T-shirts! (Or whatever they wear in high school.) Write back so we can figure something out. Because if seventh grade is going to be hard, I need my big sister around.

(Okay, I'm blushing again after writing that. This is getting super sappy.)

Love,
Evie

P.S. I do miss you.

P.P.S. How are you feeling? I looked online yesterday and it says that your baby is the size of a *watermelon* now. Ouch!

Dear Cilla,

Today was the first day of school! I was super nervous about what to wear, but Katie and Maggie agreed with my final choice—my favorite pair of jeans with this cool polka-dot shirt I convinced Mom to buy when we went to the mall last week. I wore a new pair of bright red sneakers, too. I love them.

Everyone else was wearing new clothes, too. Katie and Maggie wore matching skirts—Katie's was purple with white flowers and Maggie's was blue with white flowers. They wanted me to buy the orange one, but it wouldn't have matched my shirt. And I *really* wanted to wear my new shirt.

Miri had on new shoes that looked like they cost a bazillion dollars. She kept showing everyone the label on the soles. (Like she wasn't going to scuff up that label by the end of the day.) Miri had gone to Jamaica with her family at the end of the summer and came back really tan. Not just *Cape Cod* tan, but *tropical island* tan. Her hair is super blond now. She said it was from all the sun, but it changed like five shades, so I think she got it highlighted. Anyway, it looks silly. Miri said she got her hair braided in Jamaica, too, that she got those bright plastic beads put in, the ones that *clink clink clink* when you move your head. When I asked her where they were now, she said her mom had made her take them out before school started.

I bet she didn't even get beads. Miri lies about stuff like that all the time. They'd be against the dress code anyway. It had been a big enough deal when you wore those black spike-heeled boots to school when you were in eighth grade. You got detention and Mom and Dad grounded you for two whole weeks. It seemed like you were stuck in your room for a million years.

Now I know that two weeks is nothing. At least then I saw you at meals. I could see you smile when I gave you my crescent roll at dinner, since I knew they were your favorite. I could hear you moving around in your room, too. If I put a glass up against the wall, I could hear you flipping through magazines. At night, I could hear you snoring. LOUDLY. (Yes, I even miss that.)

I missed you the most this morning, when Mom cooked the special blueberry pancakes she makes at the beginning of every school year. She made mine in the shape of a 7 for seventh grade. (Okay, she made two 7s, since I was hungry.) She should have made an 11 for you. I think she realized it, too, because after she was done cooking mine, she stared at the empty pan for a minute. Then she got herself a bowl of cereal.

I poured tons of syrup on mine, just like you always did. So it was kind of like you were there with me.

Kind of.

Miri wasn't the most interesting thing about school, though. The girl from this summer was there! She's a new kid, after all! Her name's June and she's so nice. Until today, I hated the month of June. June was when you left. June was when our house got so quiet I could sometimes hear Dad clipping his fingernails a room away. Total grossness.

Now June's not so bad. Because she (the person, not the month!) might be my new friend. I wasn't sure if she'd remember me, but I said hi and told her my name is Evie. (I never introduce myself as Evelyn. It's way too old-fashioned. Will you introduce yourself as Priscilla at your new school?)

She *did* remember me, though! She told me her name and even said she saw me at the playground that day, when I was all the way on the other side of the park. Then we laughed about almost falling down at the carnival. When Mr. Barrett said we could choose our own seats, I asked her to sit next to me. I asked her to sit with me, Katie, and Maggie at lunch, too, but she didn't say much then. She might be shy. Or overwhelmed.

Or she doesn't like me! That could be it, because I'm not sure if you like me that much anymore, either. Is that why you haven't written back? Do you think *I* hate you, too?

Love,
Evie

P.S. I really do miss you.

P.P.S. June's hair is poufy around her head like a cloud. I bet if I reached out, it'd be as soft as a cloud, too. (I obviously didn't do that, though. That would be the most embarrassing thing ever. Way worse than tripping into someone.)

Dear Cilla,

Okay, she definitely does like me. When we had to pick partners today in art class, June chose *me*! It might have been
because she doesn't really know anyone else yet, but I'm
choosing to think it's because she thinks I'm totally cool.

The coolest girl in school. Riiiiiiight.

Anyway, our art teacher is Mr. Carlon, and even though
he's as old as Dad, *he's* really cool. He has red hair and always
wears a Red Sox hat, even though there's a rule that you can't
wear hats during the school day. Maybe that rule doesn't
apply to teachers? Or maybe he doesn't care. Because yesterday, the Red Sox were playing during class and he had the
radio on. I kept being afraid that the principal was going to
come in and yell at all of us. She didn't, though. And the Red
Sox won! I bet Alex would have been excited. He was always
wearing a wrinkled Sox T-shirt.

Mr. Carlon told us to work on a collage today. He said it
was so we could "get to know one another while I'm also getting to know all of you." He brought in a ton of old magazines:
Time, Sports Illustrated, People, Good Housekeeping . . . the
ones I always see in the doctor's office waiting room, the kind
grown-ups look at with very serious expressions. I bet you
saw a ton of those during all your appointments.

He piled them on a table in the middle of the room and

told us to take a few magazines, some scissors, and some glue. We had huge sheets of poster board, too. Then he told us to "cut out pictures that represent you and what your goals are for this school year." Each partner was supposed to use half of the poster board and then we'd see what we had in common.

I didn't think there'd be anything good in those boring magazines, but I found tons of cool photos: a picture of the sky filled with firecrackers (like the ones we watch on the Fourth of July). An old barn (which didn't look *exactly* like Aunt Maureen's, but was close). A bag of Skittles (yum!). A cross. Even a picture of a bookshelf that looked just like mine at home.

I kept peeking at June's pictures at first, to make sure I was doing it right, but then I got really into the whole thing. It was like a treasure hunt, where instead of gold doubloons I was searching for myself. Or what I thought *could* be me.

When Mr. Carlon finally told us to wrap up, I looked at June's pictures again. She had more than me, and had arranged them in a super-cool way, so they overlapped one another. For some of the pictures, you could only see the edges, a splash of bright orange or something that might have been the top of a palm tree.

But she had a bag of Skittles, too. And a picture of a unicorn (which I hadn't found, but duh! Who doesn't love unicorns?). We started talking about our favorite Skittles color (her: red. Me: purple. But only now that green is that weird sour-apple flavor. Lime was so much better. I will be sad forever that it is gone.).

June told me that her mom's friend in California (which is where she moved from) made something called a Skittles pie. It's a key lime pie with Skittles sprinkled all over the top. Which makes sense. If you can put rainbow sprinkles on ice cream, why not Skittles on pie? Or on anything!

That's when we started talking about the different things we could put Skittles on. Like pudding. Or peanut butter and jelly sandwiches. Or bacon! June suggested pasta, which made me make a face. Then I suggested meat loaf, which made June gag. We spent the rest of class trying to think of the *worst* possible combinations.

I'm glad we ran out of time, because there's no way we would have been able to present our collage to the class without bursting out laughing all over again.

It's cool to have a new friend.

Love,
Evie

P.S. I miss you.

P.P.S. The winner was Skittles and liver. Because, seriously, liver would make *anything* taste gross.

Dear Cilla,

Today's your due date. I marked it on my calendar when you left. Not with a big red circle or anything. Not even with a sparkly sticker. Just with a small black dot in the bottom right corner of the box, so small that Mom and Dad wouldn't notice it. And if they did, then they'd think I made the mark by mistake.

You left three months ago, but it feels like longer. When you left, your stomach was a little round bump peeking over the edge of your sweatpants. You complained that your feet were huge and your fingers were swollen and you threw up a lot. You still looked like Cilla, though. You could hide your bump with a baggy T-shirt and gym shorts. I could make believe you were barfing because you ate bad sushi. (Or whatever people eat when they get food poisoning. On TV it's usually sushi.)

I wonder if you look different now. If your belly has grown three sizes, like the Grinch's heart does in the movie. If that's all people can see when they look at you. It was all Mom and Dad could see before, but I could still see the real you. I saw the smile that always curves up a bit more on the right side, like you're holding in a laugh. I saw the bitten-down fingernails that you always swear you're going to grow out. I saw the annoying way you always crack your gum.

I didn't see your stomach first, even if Mom and Dad were afraid everyone else would. You were only going to have that belly for nine months, and then it'd all be over. Just a blip of time we could forget about. It could even be over now. Your baby might already be born.

I'm afraid Mom and Dad will never forget about it, though.

That years from now, the baby will be out, but the sin will still be there.

Love,
Evie

P.S. I miss you.

Dear Cilla,

It's five days past your due date now. I read online that lots of people have their first baby late, but usually not more than ten days. So I bet you'll have her soon.

I'm glad you found out her sex before you left. It made her more real to me.

But she's actually going to become *real* real soon. She'll be a person, not just an idea living inside of you. She'll have teeny-tiny little toes and crescent-moon fingernails and peach-fuzz hair. Or lots of hair. Or no hair at all.

She could look like you or she could look like Alex.

She could even look like me.

That's so weird.

I wonder if it'll hurt to have the baby. We started a puberty unit in health class this week and Mr. Quimby showed us diagrams of male and female bodies. No one believed a baby could come out of a grown woman. It seems impossible. And you're not even a grown woman yet. Or are you? Do you automatically become a grown-up when you become a mother? Or when you get pregnant?

I still can't believe that you're going to be a *mom*. I'll be an *aunt*. Will I still be an aunt after you give the baby away?

I wonder if once you see her, you'll wish you hadn't decided on adoption. Or if you'll wish you'd married Alex after all.

I don't think I could give a baby up. It's not like when I was little, and you gave me your stuffed elephant and didn't ask for it back. When you give a baby up, you can't take it back. No matter how much you miss it.

Miss *her.*

I bet you'll miss her lots. Because you wanted her at first. So did Alex. I wonder if he still does.

I remember how after your fight with Alex, you cried for three days straight. You told me that he wanted to keep the baby and raise it away from Mom and Dad. You told me that you loved him but you were scared.

Then he got angry at you for worrying about what people would think.

Then you got angry at him.

Then I didn't see Alex anymore. I didn't see happy Cilla anymore, either.

Before, we gushed over little frilly pink dresses and those cute little knit hats with the pom-poms on top. We talked about making baby food and finding day care. You talked about breastfeeding. (I ignored that part.)

After, you didn't gush at all. You didn't smile much, either. You started talking about adoption. You stopped talking about where to put the crib and started talking about what colleges you wanted to apply to. You replaced "baby" with "Broadway" and "boarding school."

I never knew if you *really* wanted all that stuff, though. It sounded like Mom and Dad's words were filtered through you. Because you looked scared when you talked about your future. You looked lost.

You looked homesick, even though you hadn't left yet.

You told me that if you didn't give her up, the baby was going to derail your life. But what if it could have been the complete opposite? What if she could have added to it? What if your fear stopped you from finding out?

I can still picture her here.

She fits. Just like you did.

Love,
Evie

P.S. I miss you.

P.P.S. When Mr. Quimby showed us the diagram of the male body in health class, Danny Donato yelled out that it was gross. Then Mr. Quimby made us yell out the body parts at the top of our lungs. He said it was "so we could become comfortable with human anatomy." Maggie said that her class was in the middle of a spelling test when they heard all of us scream out, "Penis!"

Dear Cilla,

This week in language arts we talked about description. Mr. Barrett says it's important to make sure that when we describe things in a piece of writing, we appeal to all of the five senses: sight, smell, sound, taste, and touch.

We've been describing things in our writing journals all week. I described Mom's vegetable garden and the Jesus statue in front of church. Today I wrote one about June:

June's skin is dark, like the night without stars. But the stars are in her eyes, those bright twinkling orbs. Her forehead is clear and smooth, unlike mine, which is scattered with pimples. She wears two earrings in each ear, one a golden circle and one a diamond stud. Her laugh is sometimes tinkly like a bell and sometimes snorty like the funniest thing ever. Both laughs are equally awesome.

I threw it away after class, though. I didn't know if I should use the word "awesome" in a class assignment.

Love,
Evie

P.S. I miss you.

Dear Cilla,

It's baby time! Mom got the call from Aunt Maureen an hour ago. You're having a baby today! (Or tomorrow. I'm not sure how long these things take.) Either way, you're going to be a mom!

I've decided that even though you're giving the baby up, you'll still officially be a mom. A grown-up. I still haven't decided whether I want you to tell me all about what happened (what's happening now!) after the baby's out of you. It'll either be totally cool or totally disgusting.

Mom and Dad are packing their suitcases now. I didn't know they were planning on going down for the birth, but I guess it makes sense. You're still their daughter. They should be with you right now. They want to be with you, too. I can hear them rushing around upstairs.

I argued that I should join them, but Mom and Dad do *not* agree. I begged and pleaded and promised them I'd do the dishes every single night for the rest of my life, but they still didn't change their minds. Not even when I said I'd *dry* the dishes, too. And you know how much I hate drying the dishes.

Aunt Megan is staying with me instead. I haven't seen her since before you left, when she was about to leave on a business trip to Italy. She told me she'd send me a postcard and a present, but didn't send either.

(I guess this whole "not writing to Evie" thing runs in our family.)

Not that I cared. I didn't *really* want an I LOVE ITALY T-shirt. But it'd be cool to show it to people, to know that even if I've never been anywhere exciting, that people related to me have. And that they think about me while they're there.

I wonder if you're thinking about me now. I wonder if you're in pain. I bet I could help you. I'd tell you funny stories. I'd watch cheesy reality shows with you to pass the time. I'd hold your hand, even though I bet you'd squeeze it so hard my fingers might break. That's what always happens when people have babies on TV.

I just heard the door slam. Now I hear Aunt Megan's voice. She's here already! That must mean the baby's close.

I can't wait to hear what happens! Maybe once the baby's out of you, Mom and Dad won't think of you as a sinner. Maybe the sin will be washed away, kind of like what's supposed to happen in baptism.

You'll be clean.

Love,
Evie

P.S. I miss you.

Dear Cilla,

I wonder if you're in labor still. I wonder if you got to hold your baby before they took her away. I'm wondering a lot of things, because I have no idea what's going on. Mom called this morning, but Aunt Megan hung up before I got a chance to talk. She said Mom and Dad would talk to me when they get home.

I needed something to distract myself after church (otherwise I'd be thinking about you *all day long*), so I went over to June's house. She invited me! She probably would have invited Katie and Maggie, too, but they were at this drama class at the community center. They wanted me to take the class, too, but I forgot to sign up in time.

I was okay with hanging out at June's, though. Her house is small, but it's only her and her mom. Her dad died when she was little. June told me all matter-of-factly, but I still didn't ask any more questions. That would have been way rude.

June's mom was meeting with a client (she's a graphic designer), so we grabbed a box of granola bars and some waters and went up to June's room. Which is THE COOLEST ROOM EVER. The walls are bright orange, which sounds ugly but looks totally cool, like we're on the surface of the sun or something. Then she has all these pictures of bright pink and yellow and green flowers on the wall. They're not photographs, though. Or even paintings. They look like a mixture of both, like they could be on the wall of some modern art museum.

June's mom *made* them!

After I stared around her room for about five minutes, we did a little homework. But only a little because it's Sunday and we're not *that* nerdy. Then we watched *The Force Awakens*. It was the hundredth time for both of us, but we still love it. We took turns pretending to be Rey and acted out the lightsaber fight at the end.

It was fun. I like June. I mean, as a friend.

When the movie was over, June said something weird. She said that Rey was cute. I didn't respond for a few seconds because I didn't know what to say. Katie and Maggie say that Joey's cute all the time. Katie says that Ethan from our class is cute, too. They never say that girls are cute, though, even though I definitely notice stuff like that sometimes.

It's like how Mom says that actresses on TV are pretty. Or *People* magazine has that Most Beautiful People issue every year. It's a fact. Some people are cute. Some aren't.

There's nothing weird about that.

Love,
Evie

P.S. I miss you.

P.P.S. When I got home after the movie, Aunt Megan was on the phone with Mom again. She still wouldn't tell me anything, and now Mom and Dad won't be home until early next week.

P.P.P.S. You'd better be with them.

Dear Cilla,

You weren't with them.

But you obviously know that.

When Mom and Dad walked through the front door, Dad came in with their bags. Mom came in with an empty Coke bottle and a banana peel.

They didn't have you.

They looked really tired. Mom was playing with her cross necklace, the way she always does when she's upset. I knew they probably wanted to talk to me about why you weren't home, but I didn't give them the chance. I didn't want to ask them why you were away at school, because that would mean you'd decided to stay away. Because if you really wanted to come home, you'd have fought harder.

So I ran upstairs to my room and slammed the door. Then I turned on my music super loud—*without* earbuds, ha!—and pulled my covers over my head.

I'm done writing to you. I'm only sending this letter so you'll know that. If you want to talk to me, you'll talk to me. You know where to find me.

Love,
Evie

P.S. I *don't* miss you.

P.P.S. I'm using Saint Augustine's address for this letter because Mom says you don't have an e-mail address there. I checked the website, though, and all the teachers have e-mail. So does the "custodial specialist." Is that what they call the janitor at your fancy new school? Whatever. You won't write back anyway.

P.P.P.S. Neither will I.

Dear Cilla,

Okay, maybe I'm not done writing. Because I realized something today. Something that made my chest ache. Something that made me realize I'm not the only one hurting.

I went over to June's house again yesterday. I wanted her to come here, but Mom was sick. Really sick. She spent the entire day in her room with her door closed. When I asked her if I could go, she didn't even answer me. She just groaned and sniffled.

June's aunt Ophelia was over, too. She was visiting with her baby, Nina, who was two months old. That's why June moved here from California, so they could be closer to family. Nina has the teeniest fingers and the tiniest toenails and the cutest little upturned nose. Even though she's so little, she has a ton of curly black hair. Aunt Ophelia had put a purple headband on her, too, to match her outfit.

She smelled like baby powder and sugar cookies.

Did your baby smell like that after you had her? How could you have smelled that and still given her up?

Aunt Ophelia asked me if I wanted to hold Nina. I shook my head at first, but then she held her out to me. Nina wasn't crying at all and she kept making gurgling noises, where these little spit bubbles popped out of her mouth. She was too cute to say no to.

I pretended she was your baby. I even named her in my head: Anna.

Hush little Anna, don't you cry, Evie's gonna sing you a lullaby.

Aunt Ophelia was talking to June's mom about labor. They called it "comparing horror stories." It really *was* gross. Aunt Ophelia said she had been in labor for thirty-one hours with Nina. That's more than a whole day! She said she was screaming nonstop the whole time. June's mom's story was totally different. She had June in a tub! Not in a regular bathtub, but in a special pool designed for having babies. June actually came out into the water. Isn't that cool?

I wonder how you had Anna. Or whatever you would have named her. I wonder how much it hurt.

When her mom said all this, June made a face and pulled on my arm. "Mom, I do *not* want to hear all about your bodily fluids and my smooshy face again. Evie and I have work to do."

I gave Nina one more pat on the head (I made sure to watch out for her soft spot) and left. I could still smell her baby smell in June's room. I was still calling her Anna in my head.

I was crying before we even got to June's room. When she asked me why, I started to make up some story about dust getting in my eye or having a sick grandma, but then I told her the truth. The real truth, not the fake truth that Mom and Dad forced me to tell everyone, even Katie and Maggie. And she was okay with it. She gave me a hug and squeezed me extra tight.

The hug gave me little goose bumps, which was weird. I also kept thinking about how June had said that Rey was cute. But then I decided there was nothing weird going on. It's just that I've never had such a good friend before.

A little while later, I had to pee. June's upstairs toilet was broken, so I had to use the one downstairs. I peeked in the kitchen as I walked by. I wasn't trying to eavesdrop; I just wanted to see the baby again. But Nina was sleeping in a sling around Aunt Ophelia, so I couldn't see her face.

I was surprised she didn't wake up, though, because Aunt Ophelia was complaining really loudly. All this stuff about how she was sleeping like two hours a night and how she cried all the time. How hard it was to shower and how lonely she was when her husband was at work. Mrs. Reynolds squeezed her hand and mumbled a bunch of stuff I couldn't hear, so I finally went to the bathroom.

Hearing them made me realize something: for months now, I've been thinking about me.

About me feeling alone in our house, with only Mom and Dad for company.

About me not being able to talk to you.

About me not getting to meet the baby before you gave her away.

Here's what else I realized yesterday, though: I forgot to think about *you*.

You must be even lonelier than me.

You must want someone to talk to.

You must miss so many things:

Your friends.

Alex.

Anna.

Me, hopefully.

Maybe you're depressed, and that's why you haven't written back. I keep imagining you in a cavernous room in your creepy old school thinking no one loves you.

I care. I love you.

Love,
Evie

P.S. Most of all, I miss you!

P.P.S. Do you have a phone there? I know Mom and Dad took yours away after that first big fight, but isn't there one in your room? Can you call and give me the number?

Dear Cilla,

Here's something I thought of yesterday: maybe my letters *weren't* getting through to you at Aunt Maureen's. Maybe the mailman really *couldn't* find her farm, just like Dad couldn't on our road trip.

So I'm going to hope you start writing back now that I'm writing to you at your new school. And I'm going to try to be nicer to you. More understanding.

A better sister.

Here's the deal: you don't have to come home. If you're still ashamed you had a baby or you don't want to see Alex or you're scared of what your friends will say, that's okay. You don't have to come home for good.

Can you just write back, though? Even once? Can you let me know you're okay?

Love,
Evie

P.S. Because I miss you.

Dear Cilla,

I saw Alex at the high school football game on Friday when I went with June. Well, I went with Mom and Dad (they'd signed up to sell tickets), but June came with us. We saw Alex when we were going to get food at the Snack Shack. June snuck a few handfuls of my popcorn (which her orthodontist had told her not to eat) and I snuck a bite of her hot dog. Mom wouldn't let me get one since it was Friday. June's mom doesn't care about the "No Meat on Fridays" rule, though. Do you know why? It's because June's family is atheist!

I've never known anyone who doesn't believe in God before. I didn't even think it was an option. God is real. Of course God is real. But when I asked June why she didn't believe, she just shrugged.

"Why *should* I believe?" she asked. "Where's the evidence?"

I looked at the pine trees surrounding the football field. At the moon shining in the sky. I remembered the sunset earlier that day and how a squirrel scurried across the grass when I left for school.

There's the evidence, I thought.

I didn't say anything, though.

Because I got distracted when I saw Alex. He was standing by the fence, talking to one of the cheerleaders. I don't know her name, but I think she's been over our house before for some school project you guys did together one year. He turned around right when I was looking at him and made eye contact. He jumped a little bit, like he'd been electrocuted.

Or like he'd been caught doing something very, very wrong. He ran over to me right away. "We're just friends! We're just friends!" He kept saying it over and over, like it mattered to me who he was dating.

Like it might matter to you.

Do you still love Alex? I know you guys had a big fight, but he's still the father of your baby. Even if you don't have her anymore, she still belonged to you two once.

I liked Alex. I still *do* like him, even if you guys had a fight. He doesn't treat me like a little kid.

He asked about you.

I wish I had something to tell him. Please write back.

Love,
Evie

P.S. I miss you.

Dear Cilla,

Yesterday afternoon Maggie and Katie went over to June's house for a horror movie film fest. I couldn't go, of course, since Mom and Dad are "morally opposed" to horror movies. I bet you can still picture Mom's pursed lips all those times you asked to watch one.

June told me about the movies in art class today, though, complete with creepy sound effects. She makes the best faces. She even looked pretty pretending to be a zombie.

Love,
Evie

P.S. I still miss you! Remember me? Your sister? Your sister who'd love to hear from you?

P.P.S. I bet I'll get a letter any day now.

Dear Cilla,

Mom heard me say your name on the phone this morning. Her lips pressed together like she'd tasted sour lemonade, like that time we added salt instead of sugar. I was talking to Katie and Mom made me hang up right away. When I told her it wasn't fair, she said that nothing that happened was fair. Then she went to her room and cried. The television in her room was blaring, but I still heard the sobs. When she came out, her eyes were all red and puffy, but she pretended nothing had happened. We folded our hands and said our prayers and everything was fine again.

Mom made macaroni and cheese for dinner tonight, the kind with three cheeses, just the way you like it. She made brownies, too. And cheesecake. She's turning into a cooking machine.

Mom cried after dinner, too.

Love,
Evie

P.S. I miss you.

Dear Cilla,

Mom and Dad are the worst. The absolute, probably-verified-in-a-scientific-experiment WORST.

Katie and Maggie and June are dressing up as devils for Halloween. We all went to the party store together and bought the coolest costumes—a red bodysuit with sparkles all over it, red shimmery tights, and a long tail. We even got headbands with devil horns and matching pitchforks. When we tried the costumes on at June's house, she kept flicking her tail in my face, which totally tickled.

But when I told Mom and Dad about our costumes, they said there was no way I could go trick-or-treating dressed as the devil. Like the second I put my costume on, I'm going to start worshipping Satan or something.

Don't they *get* it? Halloween is a holiday! It's for dressing up and laughing and trick-or-treating and getting candy. Lots and lots of candy. This is probably going to be one of my last years, too, so I want to go with my friends. As a devil. Not the *real* devil (who probably isn't real, anyway). A pretend devil.

Is that so hard to understand?

They are the WORST!

Love,
Evie

P.S. I miss you. I miss the voice of sanity in this house!

Dear Cilla,

In the end, we were three devils and an angel. An angel wearing a white sweater, white leggings, and a "halo" made out of cardboard.

It was the worst Halloween costume ever.

June said I looked cute, though. I didn't know what to think about that, but I guess I did look cute. At least my hair did.

Love,
Evie

P.S. I miss you.

P.P.S. Did you dress up for Halloween? If you don't want to write back, maybe you can just send me a picture? Or do they not do Halloween at your school?

P.P.P.S. I got *twelve* Reese's Peanut Butter Cups, and *two* were full-size!

Dear Cilla,

No letters. No nothing. (That's a double negative, but you know what I mean.)

I e-mailed the headmaster of Saint Augustine's yesterday. I figured that if these letters really aren't getting through to you, maybe he can give you a message in person.

He must be really busy, though, because I haven't heard anything yet.

From anyone.

It's my birthday this week, too.

Hint hint.

You don't have to buy me a present. A letter would be nice. I'd even take a postcard at this point.

Love,
Evie

P.S. I miss you.

Dear Cilla,

Happy birthday to me! Happy birthday to me! Happy birth-day to meeeee-eeeee, happy birthday to me!

Or not.

Last year, when I turned eleven, you woke me up on my birthday by bouncing on my bed and shoving a shiny red bag in my face. A shiny red bag filled with colored pens (my favorite!), two new books, and a Hogwarts T-shirt.

When I turned ten, you woke me up on my birthday by bouncing on my bed and giving me a gift certificate to the trampoline park.

When I turned nine, you woke me up on my birthday by bouncing on my bed and giving me a picture of a unicorn that you'd drawn. You didn't have any money because you'd gone to the movies twice that month.

When I woke up today, my bed was still and silent. Mom and Dad wished me happy birthday at breakfast. They didn't say anything else. Mom made scrambled eggs, which I usually love, but she'd burned them. They gave me a card they'd signed their names to (no personal message, no little doodle, not even a heart) and some book with writing prompts. Religious writing prompts.

"If you want to write, you can write in here," Mom said.

"It'll help you understand our faith's teachings better," Dad said.

I shoved it in my desk drawer and went to school. Maggie, Katie, and June had decorated my locker with balloons and streamers. Maggie bought me a book. It had two kids carrying a red canoe on the cover. I've never been canoeing before, but the book looked good. Katie got me a bracelet with four charms: a heart, a sun, a pencil, and a flower. I can add on to it, too! There's a website where I can buy new charms.

June got me a pair of earrings: little blue stones. I usually don't wear earrings, but she told me these reminded her of me and that they looked like my eyes. This made me blush, so I mumbled thank you and shoved them into my pocket. I apologized later for being rude, but she said it was okay. I put the earrings in then. They do look pretty.

Love,
Evie

P.S. I miss you.

P.P.S. Since we usually plan mine together, I also missed having a party this year. I know I could have planned it on my own, or with Mom and Dad, but it didn't feel the same.

Dear Cilla,

Mr. Carlon took us to the library during art class today. We're starting a unit on sculpture, so Ms. Manfredi, the librarian, pulled all these books for us to look through. Mr. Carlon wanted us to "feel the muse" and "be inspired by the masters." He said it in this booming voice, then pounded on his chest. Katie and I rolled our eyes when he turned away. June did, too.

Mr. Carlon may be cool, but he's also ridiculous. Maybe he should have been a drama teacher instead.

It only took me about ten minutes to page through the books that were left after the rest of the class descended on the table. I saw stuff by Michelangelo and Raphael (none of the other Ninja Turtles, though, haha), but everything looked like a bunch of clay to me.

Mr. Carlon was on the computers across the room (probably checking his e-mail), so I wandered into the stacks. Ian Mahoney and the basketball guys were in the fiction area, so I headed for the nonfiction. I looked through a book called *The Life Cycle of the Butterfly* before I got up the guts to look for what I really wanted: *Teen Pregnancy and You*.

I was kind of surprised that it was on the shelves, actually. Remember a few years ago when Mrs. Clarke from church started a petition for the elementary school to ban that book about gay penguins? And Mom and Dad signed it and went to the big town meeting? You were so embarrassed. I didn't know enough to be embarrassed then, but I definitely am now. We don't live in the Dark Ages. If penguins want to be gay, let them be gay. Whatever.

Anyway, I thought that after that, Mrs. Clarke went around in the middle of the night burning all the "controversial" books. But there it was, right next to *Teenage Sexuality: Opposing Viewpoints* and *GLBTQ: The Survival Guide for Gay, Lesbian, Bisexual, Transgender, and Questioning Teens*— everything I wanted to know about teen pregnancy. (Like I don't know enough already.)

Working up the nerve to actually take the book off the shelf took a few minutes. Maybe more. I kept looking around me and moving up and down the aisle whenever I heard giggling or rustling. (Someone was wearing corduroy pants, otherwise known as the *loudest pants ever. Swish swish swish!*) Luckily most people were over by the computers.

It took me another two minutes to open the book and look over the table of contents. I don't know what I was expecting— information on why being pregnant might make you sad? A chapter on what to do if your older sister gets pregnant, gets sent away to have the baby, and never comes back?

WHEN SHE SAYS SHE'S GOING TO.

The book was about twenty-five years old, though, and all it had was really technical stuff. Eggs, sperm, ovaries, uterus. Labor and delivery. Newborn care. Day care. I don't care about all those facts. I care about *you*.

Fact: Mom and Dad said that your labor was fine and the baby is fine and everything is fine blah blah blah.

Fact: The baby (I still think of her as Anna) is with some family that loves her.

Fact: You decided to stay at Saint Augustine's instead of coming home.

Reality: I don't know why things turned out this way. I *know* you wanted to come home. I just know it.

Stupid books.

Stupid libraries.

Stupid you.

Love,
Evie

P.S. I miss you and I hate you and I love you.

Dear Cilla,

I have to tell you something. I don't know if I should, but it's been living inside me all week. It feels like a huge rock inside my stomach. A huge rock that keeps growing.

Last week, we went out to dinner for my birthday. We went to Bianchi's, your favorite. When we got there, the host, that old guy who's worked there for about a billion years, asked if we needed a table for four. He pulled out four menus as he was asking the question, too, like he was expecting you to burst in the door any minute.

That's how much you're a part of this family. The bald guy with the nose hair knows you should be here.

I guess Mom and Dad didn't get that memo because Dad shook his head and said we'd need a table for three. The host didn't ask any questions, which I was kind of bummed about. I wanted him to ask why you were gone. I wanted him to mention you, even if he doesn't know your name.

If you weren't here, I at least wanted your name to be.

But, nope! He just gave us our menus and sat us at our regular table. He took away a chair, too. Your chair. Brought it to a table across the restaurant for this short guy with a foot-long beard. He caught me looking at him once and gave me a mean look. So I stopped.

Bianchi's still has the lasagna that's almost as big as my

head. I didn't order it, though, because I knew I couldn't eat it without you to share it with. And I definitely didn't need to bring home leftovers, since Mom's still cooking like a madwoman. I mean, she used to cook dinner and make those "in a pinch" meals for people at church, but she's turned into some supercharged chef version of the Energizer Bunny. She won't stop. Our freezer is full of frozen lasagnas, enchiladas, and soup. Cookies, too. I didn't even know you could freeze cookies!

But what I ordered for dinner isn't the point of this letter. (I got the ravioli, by the way. *So good*.) It's who we saw at the restaurant.

After we gave the waiter (the one with black hair who you always said was so cute) our drink order, a guy came up to our table. He was tall and skinny and looked like a giant string bean. He wore a thin green bean–ish tie, too. He had a big pimple on his chin and a thin black mustache that looked like a hairy black caterpillar.

Do you like my description of him? Mr. Barrett taught us about similes yesterday. Similes compare one thing to another different thing. Similes have to use the words "like" or "as," though. Metaphors don't.

You probably know that, but I still mix them up sometimes.

The man was named Peter. Dad said they played on the same Ultimate Frisbee team in college. He didn't look like an athlete, but neither does Dad. Every time he told us stories about his "glory days" at Amherst, I could never picture it.

He said he had long shaggy blond hair and practiced bare-foot. He said he could throw a Frisbee the length of a football field and from April through September his sunglasses tan made him look like a raccoon.

Now he wears suits to work and helps people file their taxes.

I don't get it.

Peter seemed to remember the old Dad, though. He clapped Dad on the shoulder, which made Dad wince. "Tommy, good to see you! It's been too long!" Then Dad got up and they did that weird man-hug where they pat each other's backs for a few seconds.

"How have things been since college?" Dad shook his head. "I can't believe it's been twenty years." They muttered stuff about how it was impossible they were so old and it just yesterday that blah blah blah. They talked about weird Ultimate terminology, like "hammers" and "spirit of the game" and "flicks." Peter asked Mom if she was still the "best baker in the whole damn country."

This made me flick (probably not the flick they were talking about, though) my eyes to Mom and Dad. I've never heard Mom swear, and I've only heard Dad say "damn" once, that time I was in the backseat and you'd just gotten your permit. You swerved to avoid a squirrel and almost crashed into the brick wall in front of Tony's Pizza.

Once it stopped being scary, the look on Dad's face—both when he realized what had happened and when he realized he'd said a swear (well, what *they* consider a swear)—was the funniest thing I'd ever seen.

Mom and Dad didn't react, though. Mom just said that yeah, she was still baking, and Dad talked about how her lemon crumble was the hit of every post-church reception.

(I bet you miss Mom's lemon crumble. I bet you miss her blueberry scones, too. And her peanut butter cookies. I bet they don't have anything like that at Saint Augustine's. I bet you get stale crackers for dessert. Or Communion wafers. Which are just as gross.)

Then Peter asked about me.

"Is this your only kid? She's a beauty."

Mom and Dad exchanged a look. That mind-reading look they do when they need to "talk" without saying a word. Then Dad said something awful.

"She's our only daughter." He put his hand on my head and smiled. Mom smiled, too. They were the fakest smiles *ever*. "This is Evelyn Jane."

I didn't know what to say, so I didn't say anything. My mouth flapped open like the fish Mom buys at the market for "No Meat Fridays." I bet my eyes looked as dead, too.

I'm *not* their only daughter. You might be gone, but you're still part of our family. Even if they're ashamed of what you did, they shouldn't deny you. That should be pretty damn (ha! I can say it, too) obvious for people who say their favorite book is the Bible.

I stared at Mom and Dad hard, like I had some magic

power that would make them correct themselves and take back their words. They didn't, though. Dad's lips were pressed so hard together they started turning white. Mom made this little choked sound like she'd been punched in the stomach. They both stared at the ground.

But they didn't say anything. It was like because you had a baby before marriage, you didn't exist anymore. That you were just—*poof!*—gone. Like you'd never been born at all.

They talked about weddings and jobs and weather and other boring grown-up stuff after that. Then Peter left. The bell on the door jingled behind him.

I feel awful for not standing up for you. I don't want to forget you. I don't want other people to forget you. I want to talk to you, and not just in these letters.

Was I wrong to tell you this? Is it going to make you feel worse? I need to tell someone, though. If I write about what happened, then it's proof you're real. It's proof you're still my sister.

Please write back with proof that that fourth chair won't stay empty forever.

Love,
Evie

P.S. I miss you.

Dear Cilla,

Today's December 17th. I looked at one of those baby websites online and there was a due date calculator. You could put in the day you got pregnant and it would figure out when you're going to have the baby. I did it backward and put in your due date. Then I fiddled with it until I got the date I wanted.

Today is one year since you conceived. Since you got pregnant. You've only been gone since June, but a year ago today is when everything changed, even if I didn't know it.

A lot of things can change in one year. A lot of things can change in six months. Like me. Here are the most obvious ways I've changed since you left:

1. I'm taller. Only by an inch, but being 5 feet is way better than being 4'11". I had to get new pants because my socks were showing. All my socks are boring white, too, nothing like the cool print and stripey ones everyone at school has.

2. I started playing the flute. I'm not very good and sometimes it sounds like a cat when someone's stepped on its tail, but I can play "Baa, Baa, Black Sheep" and "Twinkle, Twinkle" *AND* read

music now. Mrs. Harper taught us tricks to re-member which letters go with which lines and spaces.

FACE: Like a face. (Duh.)

EGBDF: Every Good Boy Deserves Fudge.

The official name for the tricks is a "mnemonic device." Like how you remember the names of the planets by saying "My Very Eager Mother Just Served Us Nectarines." There are lots of other mnemonic devices, too. Maybe you're learning some at your school. That's cool to think about. Like how sometimes people look up at the stars and think that someone far away is staring at the same ones.

3. I think I might be allergic to raspberries. Every time Mom brings her raspberry pie to a church re-ception, the back of my throat starts itching. Not a lot, but enough to make me stick my tongue back there and wiggle it around. Last week I didn't eat the pie and Mom got mad at me.

4. I don't really talk to Mom and Dad anymore. Par-tially because I don't want to and partially because they're too distracted to talk to me much lately. I ask them to give me a tissue and pass the remote. I

tell Mom I need a ride to the store to get new Chap-Stick. I tell them about my day, but only the stuff that happened in class. I don't tell them anything important. I don't tell them about June or how in art class yesterday she kept flicking paint at my nose. Then I flicked red paint at her nose, so we both looked like Rudolph the Red-Nosed Reindeer by the end of class. I don't tell them how much I miss you. I still pray with them, but sometimes I'm not sure if God is hearing what I'm saying.

5. There's one more thing that might be different about me. I can't tell you yet, though. I'm not even sure about it myself.

Love,
Evie

P.S. I miss you.

P.P.S. Mrs. Harper told us that when she was younger and Pluto was still a planet, the mnemonic device they used was "My Very Eager Mother Just Served Us Nine Pizzas." We're having pizza tonight. Mushroom pizza. You hate mushrooms. I think that's why we get them now. I'd rather have you than mushrooms, though.

Dear Cilla,

I still haven't heard back from the headmaster. Or from you. Maybe Dr. Locke isn't checking his e-mail because of winter break. But if Saint Augustine's is closed for vacation, where are *you*?

I was going to ask Mom and Dad about your Christmas plans the other night, but when I knocked on their door, I heard Mom crying. When I peeked through the crack, I saw her going through the trunk at the end of their bed, where she stores all our baby stuff. She had tons of your old stuff piled on the bed: a pair of tiny sneakers, your frilly white baptism dress, even a gross chewed-on pacifier. Piles of papers and drawings you made when you were little. I backed out of there before she saw me, but not before I saw her face. It was red and blotchy, like she'd been crying for hours.

I don't understand. Why would Mom be crying so much if she was so ashamed of having you around? Maybe she misses you, after all. I'm going to let Mom and Dad calm down, and then ask them about you. Not about only Christmas, but about whether you can come home for good.

Love,
Evie

P.S. I miss you.

Dear Cilla,

I waited a few days to ask Mom and Dad. They were finishing up the rosary before bed, so I ducked back around the corner, but it was too late. Mom put her beads on her Bible and Dad wrapped his around his fingers. Mom was wearing this awful robe she bought herself last month. It's long and black, with pearl buttons on it. She looks like a nun. Or a ninety-year-old widow.

I remember when she used to wear fun clothes. Like those bright red leggings she had with the white polka dots on them. Or the purple bathing suit Dad said made her look like Marilyn Monroe. Dad laughed when I said I didn't know who Marilyn Monroe was and told me she was some beautiful movie star from the old days. Then he twirled Mom around, bent her practically upside down, and kissed her. He only stopped when you ran down to the ocean, got a pail of water, and dumped it on their heads.

Everyone on the beach thought we were the weirdest family ever.

I'd rather be weird than . . . *this*, though. Whatever "this" is.

I'd rather be soaking wet and covered in gritty wet sand and seaweed than living in a land of black robes and pearl buttons and sadness.

They *looked* sad when they finally noticed me. Annoyed, too. I started my speech anyway. I was sure I could convince them it was time for you to come home. And that if you're the one staying away on purpose, then it's their job to bring you home.

Nothing came out right, though.

When I talked about how you were family, Mom teared up. When I talked about how you've been away long enough, Dad's face turned into a mask of stone. Then I started yelling. About how they're not being fair to you or me and how they weren't fair to your baby by making you hate it. That you wanted to keep it at first and that everything is their fault.

That's when Dad lost it. I've never heard him yell so loudly. That's when Mom started sobbing. Dad teared up, too, I think, but that may have been from all the screaming. I had no idea what was going on, so I ran out of the room.

I'm crying, too. That's why this page is all smudgy. I hope you can still read it okay. I love you. I tried.

Love,
Evie

P.S. I miss you.

P.P.S. I'm not giving up.

Dear Cilla,

It's Christmas Eve. It's Christmas Eve and you're not here. I wonder if lots of other girls are staying at school with you, or if you're the only one. Maybe lots of students board at Saint Augustine's over winter break. Maybe you sing carols and decorate a Christmas tree in the lobby. Maybe you're having a huge feast, like they do at Hogwarts at Christmastime.

Maybe you're alone in your room.

There are too many maybes and only one truth: I *don't* know what you're doing right now.

Nana's special lace tablecloth is on the dining room table, the one you spilled gravy all over when you were my age. The spot is still there in the middle, but Mom didn't put a poinsettia plant over it this year. When I asked her why not, she shrugged and mumbled something I couldn't understand.

The Christmas tree is up, but we didn't decorate it. Not two weeks before Christmas, like we usually do. Not even one week before. The branches are draped with colored lights, but the decorations are still in the attic.

No paper snowflake that you made in kindergarten, with a picture of your gap-toothed smile peeking out from the center.

No plastic Elmo.

No porcelain rocking horse, the one Mom always put at the tip-top of the tree so no one could break it.

We don't even have a real tree.

Yeah, you read that right. We didn't go to the tree farm this year. I kept waiting for Dad to drag me out of my bed on some cold, snowy Saturday morning and stick a to-go cup of Dunkin's hot cocoa in my hand. Then drag me through a field in search of the perfect tree. Where Dad would notice every tree's imperfection:

"Too tall."

"Too few needles."

"Too *many* needles."

"The branch-to-ornament ratio would be insufficient."

Then we'd roll our eyes and Mom would spot the perfect tree and run over and hug it tightly. She'd turn to Dad with that huge smile of hers (the one I haven't seen since you got pregnant) and he'd agree it was perfect.

Maybe we didn't go this year because you weren't here to roll your eyes with me.

So we have a plastic tree in our living room. A plastic, doesn't-smell-like-anything Christmas tree without a single decoration on it.

We have a stained tablecloth that nobody took the time to cover.

And we have about seven million pounds of food. Because it looks like Mom made dinner for three hundred instead of three.

I hope the food at Saint Augustine's is good. Merry Christmas Eve, Cilla. I love you.

Love,
Evie

P.S. I miss you.

Dear Cilla,

Mom and Dad got me a doll for Christmas. A doll. Like I'm five years old instead of twelve. Mom said it was a "limited-edition, special collector's edition" doll of *Anne of Green Gables*, my favorite book. And yeah, it is. And yeah, I love that book. But it's still a doll.

Maggie got five bottles of nail polish, a dress for her voice recital, a sleeping bag for arts camp this summer, and a new phone from her parents.

Katie got shoes, pink leggings, and a new pair of skis.

(We called each other right away to compare gifts, like we always do. I'm going to see June tomorrow, so I'll find out what she got then.)

I got a doll. (Oh, and five Hershey's Kisses in my stocking. The wrappers looked wrinkly, too, like Dad had pulled them out of his pocket at the last minute.)

Then I got to go to church. I heard words like "grace" and "forgiveness" and "rebirth" and "love." I heard Father O'Malley's sermon about how the birth of a baby transformed the world. I kept giving Mom and Dad these super-meaningful looks, but they didn't notice at all.

Because the only transformation that happened in our house was a bad one.

And now the only baby here is a collector's edition one meant for a little kid.

I hope you had a better day than I did.

Love,
Evie

P.S. I miss you.

P.P.S. To make the day worse, I caught Mom crying again. I didn't feel bad for her, though. If she's sad that you're not here, she shouldn't have made you feel like you don't belong.

Dear Cilla,

Things June and I have done so far on Christmas break:

Watch the first season of *Star Trek: The Next Generation*, this old science fiction show her mom loves. Then argue about which episode was our favorite.

Go to the roller rink the next town over and skate in circles with the elementary school kids. (Our excuse was that we were going with June's little cousin Iris, but that was totally a cover story. We wanted to go anyway. It was so much fun. And I only fell once.)

Play with June's karaoke machine in her bedroom for about three days straight. (That was her Christmas present.) Even though June and her mom don't believe in Jesus, they still celebrate Christmas. Which seems kind of weird to me, but I didn't say anything. At least *their* tree is decorated.

Go sledding on the big hill behind the high school. Everyone from school was there because it was the first big snowfall of the year. We took our snow tube and June's toboggan and switched off about a hundred times. Then we went back to her house for hot cocoa (her mom puts in tons of marshmallows) and chocolate chip cookies.

It was the best vacation ever.

Love,
Evie

P.S. Even if it was the best vacation, I still did miss you. Remember last year when you and Alex let me tag along when you guys went to the movies? At the scary part, I threw my popcorn in the air and a bunch of it went down the back of Alex's coat. We laughed so hard the manager threatened to kick us out.

P.P.S. I miss things like that most of all.

Dear Cilla,

Something weird happened yesterday. Something that I was going to mention in my last letter, but then chickened out. I kind of want to chicken out again, but I'm going to force myself to write it. Because I'm confused. Really confused.

During one of our sledding runs yesterday, I wiped out. Like "did a somersault in the air and then face planted into the snow" wiped out. It was totally embarrassing. There must have been a bump I didn't see. Either that or the universe hates me. Vivek was right next to me, but he just laughed his high-pitched laugh and started to climb the hill again. He didn't even check to see if I was okay.

June coasted down a second later. She didn't hit the invisible bump. But she did run over right away and ask what was wrong. So I showed her my ripped mitten. And pointed to my side, which felt like someone hit it with a baseball bat.

Then June pointed to my face, which I hadn't noticed was bleeding. But she didn't just point to my face. She touched my face. The scratched-up, bloody bit.

It hurt a little bit, but that's not why I flinched. I flinched because June was touching my face. With her fingers. I shivered, too, but that was probably because my hat fell off when I wiped out.

June flinched, too, and pulled her hand away.

We went up the hill to get a Band-Aid at the Quick-Mart next to the high school. I kept sneaking peeks at June, but she didn't say anything else. And once, when I peeked at her, she was peeking at me, too.

Love,
Evie

P.S. If you were here, I wouldn't miss you and you could help me figure out what's going on with June. ~~She was almost acting like~~

Dear Cilla,

Mom finally met June this morning. It didn't go so well. I'd been so excited, too. It was June's first time at our house, and I really wanted her to like it here.

It wasn't awful, but it *was* awkward. Totally awkward.

Mom came out of her room (there was a *House Hunters* marathon on and she'd been holed up in there all day) when we were eating a snack at the kitchen table. Mom looked kind of dazed, so I introduced her to June.

Mom said how nice it was to meet her, that she'd heard so much about her—all that polite stuff she says to everyone at church. She didn't look June in the eyes, though, which I thought was totally rude.

That wasn't the rudest thing Mom did—because then she asked June THE QUESTION. You know, the question about what's *obviously* the most important thing in the world.

Mom: So, June. I didn't see you at church this morning. Do you go to Saint Patrick's?

Me: (internal screaming and pulling out my hair)

June: No, ma'am. My family doesn't go to church.

Mom looked surprised. Not mad really, but disbelieving, like June had told her she didn't like chocolate or something. Obviously Mom has met non-Catholic people before. But I don't think she expected *me* to hang out with someone who didn't go to church.

I mumbled something about having stuff to do and pulled June into the living room. I'm not *ashamed* of June, but I didn't want Mom to find out she was an atheist. They'd think she was the spawn of the devil or something. They'd run her out of town with pitchforks.

At least Mom let us leave without dumping a vat of holy water on June.

When June and I went into the living room, she was so surprised that she stopped walking. I almost bumped into her. I'm so used to our house that I forget it probably looks weird to other people. Especially when it's their first time here.

The nativity set isn't *that* weird, especially since June doesn't know we keep it up all year long. But the crucifix over the mantel and the bloody picture of Jesus on the cross are definitely creepy. I forget about them sometimes, since they've always been there. Since church is such a big part of my life. Since basically our entire town is Catholic.

But everyone isn't Catholic.

Not everyone believes in God.

I guess June doesn't care that we *do*, though, because after she blinked a few times at our Jesus decorations, she kept walking toward the TV like everything was normal.

She's nice like that.

Having June here made me look at things differently, though. Why *do* we have a bleeding man on our wall? Mom makes such a big deal about how I'm not allowed to watch horror movies because they're "inappropriate," but we talk about a dying thirty-three-year-old man all the time. Mom doesn't let me read about zombies, but I hear the resurrection story every single year.

It doesn't make sense.

Love,
Evie

P.S. I miss you.

Dear Cilla,

It's the first day of the New Year. Last night I went to a party at Katie's house. Mom and Dad let me go, even though there was a special New Year's Mass this morning. They just made me promise that Katie's parents would drop me off at church at nine o'clock. Mrs. Foley wasn't a big fan of that idea, so Mom agreed to pick me up. I bet Mrs. Foley wanted to sleep in. So did I! I wish I was an adult and could skip church whenever I wanted to.

Maggie slept over, too. (June would have, but she was sick.) Maggie brought the brand-new sleeping bag she'd gotten for Christmas. It's shiny and maroon with silver zippers. I still have my ripped Cinderella one from when I was a kid. I almost don't fit in it anymore, but I felt weird bringing yours. Like it needed to be at home in case you came back. Not that you'll come home and need a sleeping bag. I feel like that about all your stuff, though. I haven't touched the snowflake necklace I used to borrow all the time.

Katie's younger brother, Ben, hung around us all night, but he wasn't even that annoying. He kicked our butts at board games. We played Blokus and Settlers of Catan and Twister, then ordered Chinese food. The Foleys poured glasses of sparkling apple cider into fancy wineglasses and handed them out on little trays. They had a "make your own ice cream sundae" bar, too, with three different flavors of ice cream (vanilla, strawberry, *and* mint chip), crushed Oreos, mini M&M's, sprinkles, whipped cream, and cherries! Ben is allergic to nuts so they skipped those.

Ben went to bed at ten (he fell asleep on the couch and Mr. Foley carried him upstairs), and the rest of us watched the ball drop in Times Square. We blew noisemakers and wore party hats and threw confetti. The Foleys love New Year's.

We used to, too. Remember when I was seven and you were eleven and Mom and Dad rented out the sports center across town? They invited all their friends from college and church and convinced the management to crank the heat up to eighty degrees? I wore my favorite purple-striped shorts (I was so sad when I grew out of those) and a tank top and you wore that yellow-and-white sundress that ripped before you got a chance to hand it down to me. We played soccer and kickball and basketball all night long and went home with "turf stains" all over our knees.

That was awesome.

The next year was awesome, too, when Mom and Dad decided that one year of "Summer New Year's" wasn't enough. Everyone in my class thought I was the coolest for inviting them to a bathing suit and ice cream sundae party.

(Not so awesome—when you ate three huge sundaes in a row and barfed all over the living room couch. I couldn't look at ice cream for the next month. Ew.)

Dad was wearing a winter coat when he dropped me off

at Katie's, though. No cheesy Hawaiian shirt and no sunglasses. The heat at home was set to a normal sixty-seven degrees and there were no inflatable flamingos on the porch.

No one was feeling very sunny this year. Especially me, even though Katie and Maggie wouldn't stop trying to get me to blow those annoying noisemakers. I pretended to have fun and cheered when the ball dropped, but I was secretly glad to go to sleep, even in my old sleeping bag on Katie's hard floor.

I'm glad to say good-bye to this last year, but I don't want to say hello to the new one. This is my first New Year without you at home. There's nothing about *that* I want to welcome.

Love,
Evie

P.S. I miss you.

Dear Cilla,

Katie and Maggie want me and June to try out for the school musical with them. Mrs. Harper told us about the show today during music class and they're sooooo excited. Auditions are at the end of the month and we're doing *Beauty and the Beast*. I've seen the animated Disney movie about a million times, but never the musical. I bet they're pretty similar, though.

I'm nervous, but I think I want to do it. Here's the problem: We need a parent's permission, and I'm afraid to ask Mom and Dad. You met Alex while you were doing the high school musical. What if talking about *Beauty and the Beast* makes them remember what happened and they get all mad again?

June came over after school again yesterday and we made oatmeal raisin cookies together. We used Mom's recipe, but Mom didn't help us. She did sit in the kitchen the whole time, though, reading a book.

Well, kind of reading a book. She kept staring at us. It was super weird.

I'm not used to Mom being home so much. I'm used to her shuttling you all over town. But now you're gone. And Mom is here. *A lot.*

Having a parent around when you're hanging out with a new friend is totally awkward. Not that June is a "new friend" anymore. We've known each other for four months now.

More if you count the times we saw each other over the summer. I talk to her more than Katie and Maggie lately, especially after all that time hanging out over winter break.

The cookies turned out awesome. I wish I could send one with this letter, but the envelope isn't big enough.

Love,
Evie

P.S. I miss you.

P.P.S. Things are back to normal after all that weirdness on the sledding hill. Which is good. Definitely good.

P.P.P.S. June told me that the next time I go over to her house, she'll show me a horror movie. A really gross one with a monster and a chain saw. It sounds scary, but also awesome. And Mom and Dad will never know!

Dear Cilla,

Your baby is four months old now. I read an article about what babies do at four months. Here are some of the main things:

1. They smile and gurgle all the time.

2. They start to shake rattles and grab at stuff. They grab tiny things, too, and try to put them in their mouths. So you have to be careful to pick up after yourself.

3. Their vision gets better. They used to see blurs and blobs and now they see colors.

4. Their eyes follow you around the room.

5. They start to make sounds. Sounds like "mama" or "dada."

I keep thinking about what it'd be like if you hadn't gone away. If you hadn't gone away and you'd decided to keep the baby. You'd be living in the bedroom next to me. There'd be a bassinet next to your bed. Or a crib across the room, with a pink-and-green mobile. I bet you'd have taken down all your

Broadway posters and put up a bunch of farm animal posters instead.

Alex might be sleeping in there, too, which is strange to think about. I bet I'd get used to it, though.

There'd be a stroller in the garage. I'd take the baby out for walks while you napped, since you would have been up all night feeding her.

You'd make me change diapers all the time and I'd complain, but secretly I wouldn't mind, because I'd know you were busy with school and homework and rehearsals and your daughter.

Your daughter.

That still sounds so weird.

But she isn't your daughter anymore. She's someone else's.

Is it sad to think that she's saying "mama" to someone else? That the colors she's starting to see are on someone else's shirt? That her eyes are following someone else around the room? That she's smiling at another mom?

It's weird to *me* and she wasn't even inside me for nine months. But she was still part of me. I thought about the life she was going to have. I thought about it a lot. Then it was ripped away.

I don't get why you changed your mind. I thought you wanted to keep the baby. I thought you wanted to marry Alex. What made you change your mind?

I asked Dad about the baby once. Where she was, who her parents were now. He didn't have much to say.

"We went through an agency," he said. When I asked him which agency and how they worked, he said it didn't matter. Because the baby had another family now that wasn't us. Then he shut himself in his office for the rest of the night. I don't understand why he wouldn't even tell me the agency's name.

Maybe he didn't care.

Maybe you don't care, either.

Because all I hear from anyone anymore is silence.

Love,
Evie

P.S. I miss you.

Dear Cilla,

Mom and Dad said yes to the musical! Now that I know I'm
really trying out, I'm super nervous. I'm not a very good singer.
Not like you. I sound like a strangled bird when I open my
mouth. Maybe I can lip-synch during the chorus numbers.

I bet Maggie will get the lead. She's the only one in our
grade who takes professional singing lessons. She wants to
sing some opera song from her last recital for her audition
piece. I wish I could just do "Happy Birthday." I wonder if
that's allowed.

This is the first time the district is doing a middle school
musical. Maggie said it's because the high school one is always so awesome. They want a "feeder program," so that by
the time we get to high school, we'll *already* be awesome.

Maggie knows all about what's going to happen. Her older
sister was in *West Side Story*, last year's high school musical.
You know Hannah, though. You were still here then. *You* were
supposed to be Maria before you dropped out of the show.

"You need to pick a monologue that shows off your sense
of humor." That's what Maggie said at lunch yesterday. I was
picking at my tuna fish sandwich, trying to ignore the smell
while everyone else ate their nonstinky lunches. (Do you
have to eat fish on Fridays at your new school? Does the
entire cafeteria smell like the ocean?)

Maggie turned to Katie next. "And *you* should find something dramatic. To show how you can cry on cue." Katie looked at me. She had tears in her eyes. It was pretty cool, but definitely not something I want to learn to do. I've cried enough lately.

June said she was going to write her own monologue. It sounds hard, but I bet June can do it. She said she'll help me find a funny monologue, too. Which is good, because I haven't felt very funny lately. Do you still laugh so hard that you snort? I used to think your laugh was annoying, but I'd love to hear it again.

Love,
Evie

P.S. I miss you.

Dear Cilla,

Last night I asked Mom if she watched horror movies when she was a kid. It was going to be my lead-in to convince them to let me watch one with June. I already felt bad about my plan to sneak around behind their backs. But she shook her head really firmly (her hair swished all over the place) and said no. "All that blood and guts make me feel like I'm going to throw up."

I believed her, too. Because everything makes Mom feel sick: Reading in the car. Sitting in the backseat of the car. The Tea Cups at Six Flags. Pretty much any ride at Six Flags. So horror movies would pretty much be a barf-a-palooza for her.

That got me thinking, though. Mom and Dad were kids once, right? Teenagers, too. They must have done *something* bad. They couldn't have been born these perfect angel parents with halos hovering over their heads and church outfits on. Don't all kids have a rebellious stage?

I asked them before I went to bed. Dad was working on something for work and Mom was doing a crossword puzzle. Her pen whizzed across the grid as she filled in answers.

Every clue had an answer, every box had a letter. She knew when she was right because words matched up. She knew she was wrong when there were five consonants in a row.

I bet it's nice to have everything make sense. To understand why things are unfolding in a certain way.

When I walked into the room, they both looked up. "Have you guys ever done anything wrong?" I asked.

"Like what?" Dad asked.

That's when I started to get embarrassed. I didn't want to ask them any specifics. If I did, they might think *I'd* done those bad things. Or some of my friends had. So I backtracked.

"I don't know. Like stuff. When you were young. Stuff that . . . maybe you weren't supposed to?"

Like Cilla did. I didn't say it, but I hoped they heard it. I kept pressing.

"And people forgave you, right? Because everyone makes mistakes?"

I don't think they *did* hear it, though. Because Dad started to ask me if I'd done anything wrong. And Mom told me I could always talk to them if I had weird feelings I wasn't proud of.

"Or you could talk to Father O'Malley," Dad suggested.

Yeah, right. Like I'd talk to a priest, someone who's vowed to love only God forever and ever, about the way I'm feeling.

The way I might be feeling.

They stared at me super intently, like I was one of those hidden-picture puzzles and the next thing I'd say would reveal my secret.

They were acting like I *had* a secret.

Which I totally don't.

And even if I did, I could never talk to them.

Look what happened when you did.

Love,

Evie

P.S. I miss you.

P.P.S. I'm still going to watch a horror movie this weekend. What they don't know can't hurt them.

Dear Cilla,

I finally have a good monologue. Which is a relief, because auditions are on Monday! It's about a girl who gets a dog for her birthday and all the funny things he does around the house. It took me and June two weeks to find it, and I'm super nervous about memorizing it. I think I can do it, though. When I tried to do the monologue by memory, I only messed up three times. It's a three-minute monologue, too, so that's pretty good.

June laughed *five* times when I performed it for her. I was really nervous, but she made me feel like a comedian. We were in the basement and June sat on the couch while I stood on the fireplace like it was a stage. It was awkward at first, but then I forgot she was there. At the end, I really expected to see a dog in front of me!

June's keeping her monologue a secret until auditions. I told her that wasn't fair, but she said she wanted to surprise everyone. I pretended to be mad, but I'm really not. June's too nice to be mad at for long. Then we watched TV until Mom yelled down that it was time for me to go to CCD. (I bet you don't miss that, huh?)

You know what's weird? June didn't know what CCD was. Atheists are lucky. They don't have to go to Catholic school and sit in those uncomfortable wooden chair-desks, listening to stories about saints while everyone else is having fun.

June doesn't know the Saint Anthony prayer, either. I said it the other day when I couldn't find my science notebook and she told me I was silly for asking a saint to find my stuff.

"Why don't you just look for it?" she asked.

She makes a lot of sense. Why *do* we ask saints and God for help? Why *do* I need the Patron Saint of Lost Things to find something for me? Can't we do things for ourselves? (I really hope Mom and Dad don't find this letter. They'll kill me if they know I'm even *thinking* something like this.)

Sometimes I feel like I should tell Mom and Dad about June. About her atheism, I mean. I don't want to, though. Mom already acts strange whenever she sees June. So I can't let them know about the atheism stuff. What if they make me stop hanging out with her? I can't do that. And it's none of their business what June believes in.

Plus, even though the Bible supposedly says that all atheists will go to Hell, I don't believe it. I've never actually read that part, so maybe it's not actually in the Bible. Maybe it was a rumor someone made up that was passed down since Jesus's time. Everyone *thinks* it's in the Bible but it's really not.

Maybe.

I'll pretend that's what happened. Because June isn't bad or evil. She's nice. She shouldn't have to burn for all eternity.

It makes me wonder about the Bible, though. Mom and Dad think it's super important. But it's just words someone wrote down, just like I'm writing this.

What if they *did* make it all up?

I want to erase that, but I won't. I can't stop my brain from thinking it, so I won't stop my pen from writing it. This is what else I'm thinking: *Is* God real? Because if He is, why did He let you get pregnant? Why aren't you here now?

Love,
Evie

P.S. I miss you.

P.P.S. June was wearing this maroon-and-brown-striped shirt today that made her eyes look super pretty. I told her that, but then I felt weird that I did. Is that okay to say to a girl? You tell your friends when they look pretty, right?

P.P.P.S. I got in trouble in CCD today for "daydreaming."

Dear Cilla,

I didn't get a callback. I didn't do awful, but I didn't do amazing, either, not like Maggie, who sang her opera song. Everyone clapped when she finished. Miri sang "I Dreamed a Dream" from *Les Mis* and was better than that girl from the movie. June and I decided to do a duet. We sang "A Whole New World" from *Aladdin*. She was Jasmine and I was Aladdin. I wanted to be Jasmine at first but June's voice is higher, so she won. Not that it mattered anyway. I sounded like a screechy cat.

No one laughed at my monologue, either. Well, except June, but I already knew she thought it was funny. That's okay, though, because I was the only one who laughed at hers. She talked about some car trip her family took when she was younger and how they ran out of gas and were stuck in the middle of nowhere when this guy dressed as a birthday party clown stopped to help them. I laughed because I know June used to be afraid of clowns and I could totally picture her freaking out. I don't think anyone else got it, though.

Whatever. We don't need to be in the musical. We'll have way more fun on set crew. June convinced me to sign up after the callbacks list was posted. There was a blank sheet of paper on the bulletin board next to it calling for volunteers. We're going to build and paint the sets and be in charge of the *entire* stage the night of the performance. Which is way better than stressing out about memorizing a bazillion lines and having everyone know how bad of a singer I am. Plus I'll get to spend tons of time with June.

We volunteered to create the logo for the cast and crew T-shirts, too. June's mom is going to help us. I can't wait!

Love,
Evie

P.S. I miss you.

P.P.S. Write back soon! I want to hear about all the stuff you're doing at school. Do they have activities there? Is there a musical? I wish you hadn't decided to drop out of *West Side Story* after you got pregnant. You would have been an awesome Maria.

Dear Cilla,

If you were here now, we'd be sitting at the table making homemade valentines. The kind we made every year, even when you got to high school. Remember when you were a freshman and that kid in your class made fun of you for still handing them out? I forgot his name. Brett or Brad or Brandon. Something like that. I bet you remember.

It's no fun to be made fun of. At auditions, I was afraid I'd freeze up and forget all my lines or pee my pants or something. Then everyone would laugh at me for the rest of the year. I tried to think of you, though, and how you'd tell me to ignore everyone. But that's not so easy to do in seventh grade. People still talk about the time Lila Chadwick sat on a Hershey's Kiss and didn't notice until the end of the day. People don't forget things in seventh grade. It's probably better in high school.

I hope.

It has to be, or else why would you have kept making valentines, even after BrettBradBrandon called you a loser? You made them the next year, too. The big purple heart with pink lace all over it. The turquoise one with colored beads laced around the edges. The yellow one with gold sparkles. I remember you used the fancy calligraphy pen Grandma gave you for that one. She taught us both, but you were always way better than me. My calligraphy looks like a foreign language.

I remember we made cookies last year, too. Chocolate chip cookies and butterscotch cookies and sugar cookies. We slathered pink frosting all over them and I ate so many that I was stuffed by the time Mom came home from errands and Dad came home from work and it was dinnertime. But then Mom threw up her hands and grabbed one of each kind.

"One for my appetizer, one for my meal, and one for dessert."

Mom and Dad don't do fun stuff like that anymore. Dad works *all the time*. Yeah, it's tax season, but he's at work way more than normal. He doesn't even go to Ultimate practice anymore. He complains he's getting out of shape, but then just mopes around the house and watches *Star Wars* for the bazillionth time.

Mom cooks and goes to Bible study and watches those home remodeling shows. And she says *I* watch too much TV! Because of her, I can now tell you exactly what kind of shower and toilet you should get for basically every kind of bathroom.

If you didn't care about BrettBradBrandon making fun of you for making valentines, why were you so worried about people knowing you were pregnant? I know Catholicism says premarital . . . you know . . . is wrong, but that didn't mean you had to hide it. That didn't mean you had to run away. It was like we were in some magic show and all of a sudden *POOF!* you disappeared. Like Mom and Dad were the magicians and you were the rabbit they decided wasn't good enough to be in their talent show.

If you didn't agree to stay away, things would have been different. People would have forgotten about the baby. You'd be sitting next to me and we'd be surrounded by glue and beads and pom-poms. Mom would be complaining about how she's going to find glitter in the carpet for the next year and Dad would be getting ready to go to his weekly scrimmage.

Instead, Dad's at work. Mom and I ate leftover lasagna that she pulled out of the back of the freezer. (It has ice crystals all over it and tastes like tomato cardboard.) And I'm signing my name on the back of a stack of store-bought valentines with Ariel and Flounder on them. (They were the only ones left.)

Love,

Evie

P.S. I miss the glitter. I miss you.

Dear Cilla,

Were you wondering why I was still writing out valentines, even though I'm in seventh grade? It's because of Mr. Barrett. He's super into holidays and decorating his classroom. His bulletin board has been covered with shiny red paper for the past two weeks. He had us decorate little mailboxes for our Valentine's Day party and then we exchanged valentines like we were in kindergarten. We were the only class in our grade to do it.

Everyone pretended it was silly, but it was totally fun. Especially since we were also the only class to have a party. And lots and lots of desserts! Miri brought in these red-velvet cupcakes that she said were gourmet but really tasted exactly like the store mix Mom uses when she doesn't have time to bake. Joey Witter brought in pretzel sticks, which we got to dip into frosting and red sprinkles. I was supposed to bring in those peanut butter kiss things that are your favorite, but every time I told Mom about it, she kept changing the subject. Then it was too late to bring them at all. I had to be the girl who showed up with a fruit salad. One premade at the supermarket where the pineapple was already turning brown.

That wasn't the most embarrassing part, though. That happened later, after lunch. The student council has this thing called Flowergrams. Did they do it when you were in middle school? You can buy a flower and have it sent to someone you like. The eighth graders were talking about it in the hall all week. I got one for Katie and one for Maggie and one for June. They all got me one, too, but then I got another one from Joey Witter!

He smiled at me when I looked at the tag.

It was weird because I definitely don't like him that way.

So I hid his flower in my desk and kept the other three on top. He stopped smiling then.

I know that was probably mean of me, but I couldn't think of anything else to do. I don't want anyone thinking I like him.

Love,
Evie

P.S. I miss you. I hope you get my letters soon.

Dear Cilla,

Joey Witter came over to our table at lunch today. Walked right up and stood next to me. He was so close I could smell the peanut butter on his breath. He was wearing that body spray they sell by the registers at CVS and Alex practically took a bath in every day when you guys were first dating.

Joey asked me about the math homework, which was weird because he *knew* we didn't have any. He'd shouted "Woo-hoo!" in class when Ms. Pasquale told us. Joey's voice was all shaky and kind of squeaked when he talked to me, too. Then his cheeks turned as pink as bubble gum and he practically ran away.

Ugh. UGH UGH UGH. I think he *does* like me.

These are the times I wish you were here. When I could curl up on your bed and watch you do homework, then casually ask how to stop a boy from liking me. Or when I could go running with you (or bike beside you) and we could talk about *why* I don't like Joey. Katie and Maggie say he's dreamy, but I don't get it. Maybe I'm too busy choking on his body spray.

I can't ask Mom or Dad about stuff like this. They'd tell me that seventh grade is way too young to think about boys. Or they'd start freaking out that I'm going to get pregnant or something. They'd be freaking out about nothing, too, because I *don't* like boys that way yet. They smell gross and fart and burp *all the time*. Plus I don't see what's so dreamy about floppy hair that looks like it hasn't been brushed since Christmas.

You wouldn't react like Mom and Dad if you were here.

I can still go into your room and I can still ride my bike or run outside. There's just no you to do it with. No you to talk to.

Love,

Evie

P.S. I miss you.

P.P.S. And I *still* haven't gotten a letter from you.

Dear Cilla,

The postal box near school has a sign on it that says mail pickups are every day at 11 a.m. and 4 p.m. That means that one of these letters should have gotten to you. *All* of these letters should be getting to you. You're not in farm country anymore, so why haven't you written back? I mentioned a mail thief as a joke, but maybe there really is one.

Or the mailman is just really bad at his job.

I wish I wasn't in school during those times. If I didn't have school, I could stake out the postal box and solve the mystery of the missing letters. Either that or yell at the mailman.

I do have lunch at 11, though. I wonder if I could sneak out. The eighth graders do it all the time. They hide behind the teachers' cars in the parking lot to avoid the security guard and then go through the hole in the fence to the Dunkin' Donuts down the street. You can always tell which kids went because they smell like doughnuts the rest of the day. *Glazed* doughnuts. My favorites.

Miri went with them last week. She likes this guy Nolan in eighth grade. He plays Pop Warner football and Miri says he's going to be the quarterback of the high school team next year. I think she's just saying that, though. Because Nolan is really short. (He's kind of a jerk, too. Miri's the only seventh grader he talks to.)

Are you not allowed to write back? Mom said you don't have e-mail, but maybe they don't let you write letters, either. Maybe you're locked in some dark dungeon, shackled to the wall in chains! Maybe you didn't *decide* not to come back. Maybe you're a prisoner!

I think the horror movie we watched last night is getting to me. June convinced me to watch another one with her, even though the first one really freaked me out. This one was really old, but she said it was her favorite. But I couldn't get through more than a half hour without clutching June's arm. The ghost mask was way too creepy. June was nice, though. She turned the movie off right away and gave me a hug.

I jumped a little bit when she did it, and June pulled back. She hugged her arms to her chest.

"Was that weird?" she asked. "Because, um, maybe I shouldn't have."

"No, it's okay," I said. "Unless you, um, didn't want to. But friends hug, right?"

June nodded. "Right."

"Right."

We didn't say anything else about it after that, and I didn't want to watch any more of the movie, so we watched funny videos online for a while. Then I showed her your school's website.

Saint Augustine's doesn't look awful in the picture. It looks like Hogwarts, all tall towers and stone walls. Big green lawns and fancy statues. No Quidditch court, though. No Hagrid's hut, either.

Sometimes I like to pretend you're actually at Hogwarts. (Don't tell anyone I said that—they'd totally make fun of me.) I pretend Mom and Dad are the Dursleys and they sent you away because you had magical powers instead of a baby growing inside you. It's nice to think about you off having adventures with Harry and Ron and Hermione instead of learning how to be a good Catholic and missing your baby.

I wonder if Dumbledore would have used an adoption agency if the Dursleys hadn't been around. I asked Mom how adoption works last night, when she was doing the dishes. I mean, I know that parents and babies get matched up, but I don't know all the details. Like, does it cost money? What happens if the baby grows up and wants to find the birth parents? Or if the aunt wants to find the baby?

Mom told me that'd be impossible. Then she scrubbed the saucepan so hard I think she took a layer of coating off.

Love,
Evie

P.S. I miss you. Please cast a magic spell and come home soon.

P.P.S. Sometimes I pretend *my* invitation to Hogwarts is on its way, too. I haven't seen an owl yet, though.

Dear Cilla,

I have a plan!

June and I have a plan, actually. She suggested it. (She's really good at being sneaky. We've watched *three* horror movies so far without Mom and Dad finding out! I've also had three nightmares.) June decided we should stake out the mailbox. It's right across from school, though, which means anyone can see us, which means I'm *super* nervous. If any of the teachers look outside at the wrong time, I'll be in the worst trouble ever.

Grounded for LIFE. Or worse.

I need to know why my letters aren't getting to you, though.

(Because that's the only explanation. It has to be. Staying away is one thing, cutting off all contact is another. And I *know* you wouldn't do that. Know it like you used to say that Alex was your "one true love." You'd say it all swoony and breathy, like the ladies in that British miniseries Mom watches.)

We're going to leave right after language arts. No one will notice we're gone in the locker rush, and if the lunch monitors ask any questions, Katie and Maggie will make an excuse. I told them it'd be good acting experience for the musical.

They agreed right away, of course. They're obsessed with the musical. Annoyingly obsessed. It's all they talk about. When we hang out outside of school, they sing *all* the time. Thank goodness I have June.

When Katie asked where I was going, I made an excuse. Katie and Maggie don't know I've been writing to you. They don't even know what happened to you. They think the same thing as most of your friends, that you were away all summer on a mission trip and then decided to transfer. They don't know about the baby and they don't know we haven't talked.

They don't know that I miss you more than I miss candy when Mom makes me give it up for Lent.

June's the only one I can talk to about everything. I've only known her for six months, but she gets me, you know? Maybe it's because her dad died when she was little. He was hit by a drunk driver when he was on his bike and died instantly. Isn't that the saddest thing you've ever heard? June didn't cry when she told me the details, though. She said she was only two when it happened, so she doesn't remember him at all. I squeezed her hand and told her I was sorry. She squeezed it back. Her hands are really soft. Her nails are longer than mine. They were painted dark maroon that day.

Do they let you paint your nails at Saint Augustine's? I hope they do. I bet you need a little shine and sparkle in that dungeon of a school.

I'm going to seal up this letter now. If you get it, you'll know our plan has worked.

Love,
Evie

P.S. I really, really miss you. If you get this letter, can you call me? Our phone number is the same.

Dear Cilla,

Joey Witter left a note on my desk today. It had a heart on it. A dark blue crayon heart. There was one of those candy hearts taped to it, too. It said WILL YOU BE MINE? in white letters.

Joey sits two seats behind me and when I turned around he smiled all big. His hair was combed and slicked down and he was wearing a fancy button-down shirt instead of the Patriots T-shirts he usually has on. He looked weird.

Miri and Zoe were whispering earlier about how cute he was, but I didn't think so. Especially when he was staring at me like that. *And* had a piece of lettuce stuck in his teeth. I didn't know what to do. Was I supposed to eat the candy heart? I didn't want to because:

1. It was green. Green candy hearts taste like dental floss.

2. It looked hard and dusty, like it'd been in Joey's pocket for the past few days. Was I supposed to proclaim my love for him? Because I definitely don't love Joey. I don't even really like him. All he talks about is football and fishing. Fishing is gross. It's all guts and worms.

So I ignored him, just like I've been avoiding him when he tries to talk to me in the hallway. I didn't even smile. So *he* stopped smiling. I hope he finally got the message.

I feel kind of bad for being mean, but not too bad. Because if I was going out with Joey, then I wouldn't be able to go out with anyone else. *If* I liked someone else, I mean.

Love,
Evie

P.S. I miss you.

P.P.S. Tomorrow is the Great Mailbox Stakeout!

Dear Cilla,

Well, we *tried* to do it. We had a plan:

STEP ONE: When the bell rang, we'd split up. June would walk toward the bathroom and I'd head toward my locker. That way, Mr. Barrett wouldn't see us leaving together.

STEP TWO: We'd meet in front of the gym. There's a foot of snow on the ground, so whatever class had gym that day would definitely be inside. Then we'd sneak into the parking lot and hide behind the teachers' cars all the way to the street, just like the eighth graders do. Only instead of going to Dunkin' Donuts, we'd run across the street and hide behind a bush.

STEP THREE: When the mailman came, I'd hand him the letter and make sure he put it in his bag. Then I'd tell him about *my* missing letters and demand he open up the mailbox so I could check for a false bottom. I'd also ask him if he knew of any suspicious behavior in the area.

STEP FOUR: He'd *really* mail my letter to you. Then you'd write or call me right away. We'd live happily ever after!

That was the plan, anyway. Steps one and two went great, even though it was snowing pretty hard by the time we got to the parking lot. June had forgotten her winter boots, too. She moved to Massachusetts from California, and I think she forgets that winter isn't just an idea anymore. I darted from car to car, but she kept slipping all over the place. She almost fell once, but I reached out and grabbed her arm. Then she grabbed *my* arm and we both fell on our butts. It hurt at first, but then we looked at each other and started laughing.

When June and I finally made it to the bush, it was snowing even harder. I kept looking back to make sure there weren't any teachers following us. June kept looking at her watch. She's the only one in our grade who wears a watch. Isn't that cool? All the other kids check their phones, but June is different. Her watch is pink, with a navy blue face. The hands of the clock are thin arrows.

I started worrying at 11:15. If a lunch monitor was going to notice we were gone, they'd definitely do it by then. By 11:20, my hair was wet from all the snow. By 11:25, we had five more minutes in our lunch block and the mailman still hadn't come.

So we left. I could see the mailbox from class when the mailman drove up at 11:47. Forty-seven minutes late! Mr. Barrett asked me why I was looking out the window and I made some excuse about the snow. That was when he asked me about my wet hair. He asked June about hers, too. Luckily he bought our excuse about a water bubbler malfunction.

So I don't think we'll be staking out any more mailboxes. Just to be safe, though, I'm going to find somewhere else to mail my letters from now on. I should have thought of doing that earlier. So if this is the first letter you've ever gotten from me, write back as soon as you can. Or call me. If you don't want to talk to Mom and Dad, you can let the phone ring two times and then hang up. I'll pick up the next time it rings. It can be our secret code.

If this doesn't work, I'll have to find some other way to get in touch with you. I'll have to take *drastic measures*. (I heard someone on a TV show say that once. It sounds super dramatic and serious. But you know what? This *is* serious.)

Love,
Evie

P.S. I miss you.

Dear Evie,

Don't worry about me. Mom and Dad and I all agree that going away to school was the best decision. My baby is happy with another family and I don't want to think about her anymore. I don't want to write about her, either.

I need some time alone, though. Can you stop writing these letters? Maybe forget about me for a while?

Love,

Cilla

Dear Cilla,

No, I won't forget about you for a while. You're my sister. My big sister. You're the one who taught me how to knit. (Not Mom, whose scarves always turn into some weird braid-pretzel-looking thing.)

You're the one who taught me how to put on lipstick. (Not that Dad will let me out of the house wearing anything more than ChapStick.)

You're the one who told me where Mom and Dad hide all our Christmas presents. (Even though the one year I got up the nerve to look, Mom almost caught me looking in her closet and I had to make up some excuse about bringing in her favorite sweater for some sort of ridiculous "Introduction to My Parents Show-and-Tell." I don't know if she believed me or not, but I never risked peeking again. No way was I risking sitting through Mom's honesty lecture. It's even longer than her "no swearing" lecture.)

So no, I'm not going to forget you for a while. You might want to forget about what happened, but I don't.

I'm *not* ashamed of you. So I'm going to keep on writing like everything is normal. Like you're on a vacation. Or studying abroad in Italy. Or France. I'll pretend you're busy eating croissants and wearing berets and hurting your neck looking up at the Eiffel Tower.

You can stop writing, but I won't. You're still my sister. You may have typed this letter, but you still signed your name. There's still a heart over the *i*. You still love me. I still love you.

Love,
Evie

P.S. I miss you, too.

Dear Cilla,

You might not want to talk to me, but it *is* your birthday. Which means I'm going to make you a card, like I do every year. It means I'm going to make you a present, too. I have enough money to buy something decent, but I decided to make you something instead.

Because you're not going to think about me when you see a boring old gift card on your desk. Or when you put on a shirt that a million other people bought, too.

But this bracelet is one of a kind. No one else has ever strung this exact same combination of beads in the whole history of the universe. (I hope.) I made this bracelet just for you. It's pink and purple, your favorite colors, and has a heart charm on it.

Please think of me when you wear it.

Then write back again. And say something sane this time.

Love,
Evie

P.S. Even if you're completely rude, I still miss you.

P.P.S. Happy birthday!!!

Dear Cilla,

Today's Ash Wednesday. Mom and Dad made me skip school this morning to go to Mass, even though it's not even a Holy Day of Obligation. Which meant I had to wear that ugly black smear on my forehead the rest of the day. There are lots of other kids in my grade who go to our church, but no one else's parents make them go to church on a school morning. Or wear dirty ashes on their face all day long.

They wear *real* makeup instead.

At least I missed our science test. I have to make it up tomorrow after school, but now I have more time to study. I'm writing this at lunch. June is absent today and Katie and Maggie are rehearsing their lines. I could help them, but they keep giggling and talking about funny stuff that happened during rehearsal. I have no idea what they're talking about and I can only fake so many laughs before I go crazy.

Mom told me last night that she's glad I'm doing set crew. She said it'll keep me out of trouble. When I asked her why I need to keep *out* of trouble if I've never been *in* trouble, she started talking about purity and how many middle school girls have lost touch with God. That they've "fallen victim to inappropriate feelings." Then she waited for me to answer her.

I had nothing to say, of course. She was really creeping me out.

I think she's afraid I'm going to turn into you.

Love,

Evie

P.S. I miss you. One letter isn't enough.

Dear Cilla,

Katie has a boyfriend! Not just any boy, either. Ethan Gagnon! Remember him? He came to my eighth birthday party and spent the whole time picking his nose and eating it. You told me his older sister Melanie did the same thing.

Ethan doesn't pick his nose anymore. (In public, at least.) His brown hair isn't in a buzz cut, either. It's long and shaggy and reaches to his ears. He usually has one pimple (it rotates around his face, from his cheek to his nose to his forehead) and he was the first person in our class to get contacts instead of glasses.

Katie says he's cute. I don't think so, but Maggie agrees. Ethan's playing Gaston in the musical. Which makes sense, because Katie's one of the three girls who swoon over him during the "Belle" song. Katie says it's "life imitating art."

Even though Maggie is Belle, she doesn't like John Lu, who plays the Beast. Maggie likes Dominic Brescia, who goes to a different school. He takes piano lessons at the same place she takes voice lessons and their moms know each other.

Dominic goes to our church, too. Mom says he's a "nice boy."

Did Mom call Alex a nice boy when you started dating or did she always hate him? She *really* hates him now. (This is probably another one of those things I shouldn't tell you.) We saw him at church last weekend. He was with his parents and Mom totally ignored them. They were sitting in the pew behind us, too, and when the priest told us to do "Peace Be With You," Mom shook the hands of EVERYONE else around us except for the Crawfords. She even did "Peace Be With You" with Natey Bigglesworth, who had cracker crumbs all over his hands. And you know how much Mom *hates* when parents let their kids eat during church.

I tried to shake Alex's hand but Mom pulled me back so hard my shoulder hurt for the rest of Mass. I bet she would have tried to move, but the church was packed and you know how they feel about standing in the back.

Remember that time Dad caught us watching *The Bachelor* (during that hot tub scene with the girl in her gold bikini!)? He turned off the TV and gave us a huge lecture about how "media like that is a corrupting influence" and "indecent behavior" blah blah blah.

(Like he hasn't seen Princess Leia in that gold bikini five zillion times.)

I think Mom and Dad think Alex is a corrupting influence. Except they can't turn *him* off. He still lives in our town and he still comes to church. They can't send *him* away.

Did he corrupt you, though? That's something I've been thinking about a lot lately. Can you control who you like? And if you like someone a lot, is it really so evil to follow your heart?

What did you like about Alex? Katie says she likes how

good Ethan is at baseball. Maggie likes how Dominic plays the piano. I don't like any boys, though. Maybe if you tell me what you liked about Alex, I could find a boy who makes me feel that way.

Just not Joey Witter. Gross.

Love,
Evie

P.S. I miss you.

P.P.S. Alex was in line behind me to get doughnuts and asked how you were doing. I didn't know what to say. Maybe you could write to him, too? I think he misses you.

P.P.P.S. Maybe you could write to *me* one more time, too? I need some big sister advice. About something huge.

Dear Cilla,

What does it feel like to have a crush? I don't know if I've ever had one.

Okay, maybe when I was six I *said* I had a crush on Kermit the Frog. But I didn't know what I was talking about. All I meant was that I liked that "Rainbow Connection" song and I loved sleeping with my Kermie stuffed animal.

I've never had a real crush before, not on a boy.

Katie says she gets goose bumps on her arms when Ethan holds her hands.

Maggie says her face turns red when Dominic talks to her.

The articles I found online say that crushes make you feel nervous and happy. You get butterflies in your stomach and you can't stop thinking about the other person. Not ever.

That doesn't happen to me around boys.

That only happens to me around one person.

Please, please write back.

Love,
Evie

P.S. I miss talking to you. I even miss you kicking me out of your room because you're too *busy* to talk to me.

Dear Cilla,

I've written a lot of letters to you. So many that I've stopped counting.

You've only responded once.

Maybe you're too busy at your new school. Wearing your fancy Saint Augustine's uniform and eating fancy brunch with your new fancy friends. Trying out for field hockey or crew or whatever boarding school kids do. Going to Mass every day and turning into the perfect Catholic daughter Mom and Dad have always wanted. The one who forgot she had a baby and forgot she has a family.

I don't want you to be that daughter, though. I want you to be Cilla. The girl who plays Hangman with me on the church missal until Mom glares at us and Dad grounds us for a week for not respecting church property. The sister who sneaks me M&M's during Lent, when Mom makes me give up candy and you give up soda.

The girl who didn't judge me for being scared of the dark until I was in the third grade.

The girl who (I hope) wouldn't judge me for anything else.

Love,
Evie

P.S. I miss you, even if you don't miss me.

Dear Cilla,

In church this morning, Mr. Jenkins asked Mom how you were doing at your new school. Mom blabbed on and on about how you joined the track team and had lots of new friends and went on a Habitat for Humanity trip last fall.

I didn't know if I believed her or not. If Mom *had* talked to you about your life there. Because you totally could be on the track team. You love to run. You *used* to run. Well, before you got pregnant and started to waddle.

But I know you didn't do Habitat for Humanity last fall. You had the baby in September. There's no way you'd be banging a hammer and putting up drywall. Or whatever it's called. So Mom was totally lying to Mr. Jenkins's face.

MOM LYING IN CHURCH. This must be one of the signs of the Apocalypse.

Then they started talking about the "mission trip" you went on last summer. The one Mom and Dad said you went on when you were really at Aunt Maureen's, growing your baby.

They babbled on and on about Haiti and orphans and medical supplies. I got angrier with every word they said. It's awful that Mom and Dad lied to the whole town about your pregnancy. It's awful that they told Dad's friend they don't have another daughter.

It's not Jesus-like of them at all.

I'm just as guilty, though. I didn't tell Katie or Maggie about the baby.

I'm not ashamed of you. I'm glad you're my sister. That's why I gave Mom a dirty look and told her *she* should be ashamed of herself. Then I walked away. I knew I was being rude in church, but I didn't care. I don't care what some guy in a suit thinks of me. I don't care what God thinks of me.

I wish our religion wasn't so mean and judgy. I want to tell everyone the truth.

I want to tell them about you.

I want to tell them about me, too.

Love,
Evie

P.S. I miss you, even if *they* don't.

Dear Cilla,

Today's the anniversary of the day June's dad died. She still came to school, though. If it were me, I'd be home crying all day long. But June said she needs the distraction of school. That learning about the Pythagorean theorem and arpeggios and dissecting worms is the only thing that could keep her mind off it. She said her mom was at home, too, and she didn't want to listen to *her* crying all day long.

I didn't know what to say. I've never had anyone close to me die. Nana did, but that was when I was five. We only saw her at Christmas, too, so I wasn't that sad. Dad was. It's the only time I've ever seen him cry. Well, besides right after they sent you away. And that time I saw him looking into your room on Christmas Day.

June didn't seem to want me to say anything, though. She didn't act like Maggie does when she's "sooooooooo upset" about something and acts all sobby and dramatic until I ask her what's wrong. She just told me about her dad and then picked up the scalpel and cut our worm open.

I don't understand how anyone can be so casual about death. Death is scary and sad. It's even sad when it's a slimy gray worm that gave its life for science. (That's why I made June do all the cutting.)

But maybe it's different when you don't remember the person, even if it is your father.

I still made sure June knew I was there to talk, though. I shared half my brownie with her at lunch and told her a really cheesy joke to make her smile.

What did the hat say to the hat rack?

You stay here. I'll go on ahead!

Yeah, I know. It's awful. But it was *so* awful that it made June giggle. And that was the whole point.

I gave her a hug after class (after washing my hands, of course. Worm guts = ew!). Because friends give hugs. We decided that last month.

June held on for an extra-long time, though. She squeezed me really tightly, too. It was probably because she was upset. She'd probably hug anyone like that.

Right?

Love,
Evie

P.S. I still miss you.

P.P.S. June smelled like vanilla and coconuts today. My favorite scent used to be your gardenia perfume, but now I think I've changed my mind. June said she bought her lotion at the mall, so we're going to go there together this weekend.

Dear Cilla,

Last night I watched the Celtics game with Dad on TV. It was a super-close game, and they won with two seconds left with a three-point shot.

Remember that time Dad's friend gave him tickets to a game and he brought us into Boston with him? We rode the T in and he let us buy pizza and nachos and those big soft pretzels you love so much. We sat in the tip-top seats, so the players looked more like action figures Ben plays with, but we could still see what was going on.

Even though I thought it was boring (I *still* think it's boring), you looked so happy. So did Dad. You guys kept comparing statistics and talking about the playoffs. You high-fived each other every time the Celtics scored. Dad was so happy he didn't even notice that the old guys behind us were swearing.

Maybe that's what Heaven's like. Doing the things and watching the things that you love all the time. Being with the people you love, too. Even if I get confused about God sometimes, Heaven is a pretty cool idea. In Heaven, I'd have an unlimited supply of books. There'd be a huge kitchen so I could bake whenever I wanted and you and June would be there right beside me.

Last night was different. Dad kept biting his lip. He didn't even seem happy when the Celtics were leading by *twenty* points at halftime. When your favorite player got a slam dunk, he looked like he was going to cry, even when I tried to give him a high five.

Last night wasn't heavenly at all.

Love,
Evie

P.S. I miss you. I think we all do.

Dear Cilla,

Even if you're not answering these letters, it's still nice to write to you. It's nice to write your name. It's proof that you exist, even if every trace of you is gone from the house. These letters are the last thread connecting me to you, as strong and invisible as the thread on a spiderweb. (See my simile there? We're talking about topic sentences in language arts this month, but I like figurative speech way better.)

Topic sentences are the sentences at the beginning of each paragraph that say what you're going to write about. Mr. Barrett says they're important, but I don't think I agree. Why do I have to tell someone what I'm *going* to tell them? That seems silly. Why don't I just . . . tell them?

Maybe not, though. Sometimes people aren't ready to tell people things. Sometimes they like to keep it to themselves until the last possible moment, when it's bouncing around inside of them like a Super Ball and finally finds the right angle to pop out.

Maybe those people don't want to use topic sentences. Maybe they don't *want* to emphasize what they're going to talk about. Maybe they want to sneak it in there at the end, quiet and subtle, so people won't think it's a big deal. Like how maybe I like someone who I'm not supposed to like and I feel like a complete freak because of it.

And how maybe that person likes me, too. But maybe not. And maybe I have no idea how to find out.

Love,
Evie

P.S. I miss you.

Dear Cilla,

Katie and Maggie hate me. Okay, maybe they don't hate me, but I'm definitely not as cool as their new theater friends. Their theater friends can sing and dance and all have boyfriends. Their theater friends push me to the end of the lunch table and ignore me when I say anything. So even if they don't hate me, I hate them.

At least I have you. And June.

But I can't talk to June about what's going on.

Beauty and the Beast is in two weeks, so everyone is super busy. We have tons of last-minute stuff to do for set crew. We even did stuff today, on a Saturday! We finished painting the backdrops. (June and I worked on the one of the ballroom *and* the one with the forest. For the castle, we used a blue-and-yellow color scheme with gold around the edges. It looks awesome with Katie's costume. For the forest, June painted a ton of super-creepy trees and I painted about five million rocks.)

I haven't talked that much about set crew so far. I bet you've been wondering why. It's not for the same reason I haven't been mentioning church.

I don't talk about church because you know what happens there. It's the same every week. We get there super early so Mom and Dad can socialize and Mom can help set up the desserts and coffee. Mom wears her pearls and Dad wears his suit. We parade down the aisle so Mom can wave at all her friends and then we sit through a boring sermon I'm not allowed to fidget through. (Meanwhile, Julia Chen is allowed to be on her phone the whole time. It's so not fair.)

Then Mom and Dad make us sit there for an extra ten minutes to pray and say the rosary before I'm dragged downstairs to make small talk with old religious people and play Ring Around the Rosie with a bunch of snotty, juice-and-doughnut-sticky toddlers.

(Even if they force you to go to church every day at your new school, at least you don't come home with jelly stains on your pants.)

Set crew is the complete opposite. We do something different every day. Even though I was disappointed at first that I didn't get a speaking part, now I'm glad. I'd be bored saying the same lines all the time. It's way more fun to say my own words instead of the words someone else wrote for me.

Because when I'm talking to June, I love what I have to say.

Here are some things we talked about today:

1. How June *finally* answered more questions right than her mom when they watched *Jeopardy!* last night. (Mrs. Reynolds is obsessed with that show. She uses a pen as a buzzer and won't let anyone talk to her during the whole thirty minutes, not even during the commercials.)

2. Which is better, peppermint stick or mint chocolate chip ice cream.

3. Whether boogers have any nutritional value.

4. Why God isn't real.

We really *did* talk about that last one. For a long time, too. June says she can't believe in anything if there isn't any proof. So I told her about faith. I talked about how I prayed for help during tests and thanked God after. I told her about the beautiful sunsets and all those images of Mary people have seen, all stuff Mom and Dad have said before, all stuff that used to seem so real to me. But when I heard the words coming out of my mouth, they felt limp, like overcooked spaghetti. *Flop flop flop!*

June said that if she thanked God for helping her get an A on a test, it would take away from her hard work. She said sunsets have scientific explanations. She rolled her eyes when I talked about all those Mary appearances.

Everything she said made sense. Which was weird.

I'm glad no one heard us talking.

We played the Would You Rather? game at the end of set crew, when everyone else was on the other side of the stage and nobody could hear us talking. We asked each other questions like:

Would you rather spend ten minutes in a room full of mosquitoes or eat a full jar of mayonnaise?

Would you rather have the paparazzi follow you around every minute of your life or never have anyone speak to you again?

Would you rather lose your sense of hearing or your sense of taste?

This was her last question: Would you rather kiss a girl or kiss a frog?

I knew my answer right away.

And when June asked me, she had this weird expression on her face, like she was actually asking me another question entirely.

I wanted to give her my answer, but I wasn't sure if she wanted to hear it. Maybe I was reading her wrong. Maybe I was reading *me* wrong.

So I didn't say anything. I finished painting another rock and June started another tree. Then Mrs. Harper asked me to go work on something else.

Which made me happy and sad at the same time.

Love,
Evie

P.S. I miss you.

P.P.S. I'm scared.

Dear Cilla,

Forget I sent that last letter. I didn't mean anything I wrote.
Burn it. Don't tell anyone. Whatever. Forget all about it.

Love,
Evie

Dear Cilla,

I'm serious. Forget everything.

Love,
Evie

Dear Cilla,

Now I'm curious about *your* answer: Would you rather kiss a girl or kiss a frog? Have you ever kissed a girl? Probably not. The Bible says homosexuality is a sin and until you got pregnant, I don't think you did anything wrong. Anything *really* wrong, I mean. Spike-heeled boots and being late for class aren't *sins*.

Kissing a girl is definitely a sin. Well, according to Mom and Dad.

What was kissing Alex like? Katie kissed Ethan yesterday after school. She told us today. It was the first time she's told me anything important in more than a month. She dragged me and Maggie into the bathroom before rehearsal, even though Maggie kept saying she couldn't be late.

(Maggie is getting a really big head. She's Belle, not Queen of the World.)

Katie walked home with Ethan after rehearsal the other day and he kissed her behind a tree near his house. She said his mouth was all smooshy and wet and she didn't know where to put her hands. It didn't sound fun to me, but Katie said she got shivers all over her body when they kissed.

Shivers *are* pretty cool.

Maggie was mad that Katie took almost a whole *day* to tell us, but I understand. Sometimes you need to have secrets so you can figure things out.

Or maybe Katie liked having the kiss belong only to her. I like to hug some memories close so I can pull them out when I need them, like the blanket I used to drag around when I was a kid. I still have it, on the top shelf of my closet, in the very back. Sometimes, when I'm really upset about something, I pull it out and run my fingers over it. It's not as soft as before. The edges are fraying and the fabric's all rough.

It still feels comforting, even though it's falling apart.

Love,
Evie

P.S. If you do come home, I really need you to forget what I said. I'd never want to kiss a girl. Really. I promise.

Dear Evie,

Don't talk to Mom and Dad about me. I'm not coming home. I like it here. I'm making new friends and learning lots.

Bringing up what happened would only make Mom and Dad upset. They were right to be upset, too. I shouldn't have gotten pregnant. I *did* do something wrong. Me and Alex did. That's why I don't talk to him anymore. That's why Mom and Dad don't talk to him, either. He's not a good influence.

June doesn't sound like a good influence, either. I'd stay away from her. It's the right thing to do.

Stay away from me, too.

Love,

Cilla

Dear Cilla,

Stay away from June? You might as well ask the sun to stop rising in the morning!

Stay away from you? That'd be worse than a bunch of angry eagles swooping down and attacking me with their talons, over and over again! (We're learning about hyperbole in language arts today, which is when you super, *super* exaggerate something for effect.)

I'm not doing it for effect here, though. It's the truth. I can't do either of those things.

Love,
Evie

P.S. Because then I'd miss you *both*!

Dear Cilla,

The musical is tomorrow night. Maggie's super nervous, even though she did awesome at dress rehearsal today. But she told me there's some superstition that a bad dress rehearsal means a good show. She's convinced that since she rocked rehearsal, she's going to forget all her lines tomorrow. Or lose her voice. So she's been drinking tea with honey all day and doing these weird "lay-la-lee-lo-lou" voice exercises.

She sounds totally fine, but she's *going* to lose her voice if she doesn't shut up.

The set looks perfect—June and I stayed late tonight putting the finishing touches on everything. We laid out everyone's costumes in the cast room and made sure nothing we'd painted had gotten dirty. No one else on crew stayed to help us, but that was okay. It was more fun with just us. Mrs. Harper was there, too, but she was in her office the whole time, on the phone with the company that made the programs.

The programs came yesterday. June's and my design was on the front (it came out so awesome for the shirts that Mrs. Harper wanted it for the program, too!), but guess what it said at the top? BEAUTY AND THE BAST. Can you believe it? Mrs. Harper had ordered eight hundred copies, too. She was freaking out.

It was dark backstage tonight. They did a lighting check earlier, but those guys left way before us. So June and I had to turn on the stage lights while we cleaned up. It wasn't exactly being in the spotlight, but we pretended it was. We knew a lot of the lines from hearing Maggie and John rehearse, so we started joking around and acting out the last scene in the show, when Belle and the Beast dance around the ballroom.

It's the scene where they kiss, too. (Maggie didn't want to kiss John at first, because he always smells like bologna, but she eventually agreed. It *is* in the script.)

When June suggested acting out that scene, I didn't want to at first. My heart started pounding and my palms got all sweaty. It made me think of an article I read in one of your magazines, right before you went away:

FIVE SIGNS YOU'VE GOT A CRUSH ON A BOY

1. You can't stop thinking about them.
2. Your heart races anytime you see them.
3. Your palms sweat.
4. You stumble when you speak.
5. They make you feel alive.

I remember the tips because I read the article a bunch of times. I wanted to remember it in case I ever felt that way. So I'd know when I met the right boy.

The article was wrong, though. They should have changed a word in the title. Because when June/Beast whirled me around backstage, everything on that list happened.

I finally knew that it was real.

I have a crush on a girl.

I'm a sinner like you.

Love,

Evie

P.S. I miss you.

P.P.S. Not for long, because I'll probably be joining you at school soon.

Dear Cilla,

I know I'm not supposed to be writing about this. I'm not supposed to be thinking it or feeling it. But just one time, for this one letter, I want to be excited. I want you to imagine me squealing and shrieking and twirling around my room. I want you to do that and *not* disapprove. I want you to be happy for me.

Because when I was dancing with June, she was smiling back at me the whole time.

I think she likes me, too.

Ahhhhhhhhhhh!

Love,
Evie

P.S. I do miss you, but right now I'm way too happy to be sad!

Dear Cilla,

I know you said that June is probably a bad influence, but you can't really mean that, right? I know you'd like her if you met her. I wish you *could* meet her.

I don't understand why you said all that stuff about her, though. It doesn't sound like you. You're not usually so judgmental. Even though our religion basically teaches us to judge people. Or to judge ourselves.

Thou shalt not do this. Thou shalt not do that. Thou shalt not do *anything*.

What if we *want* to do this or that? Isn't it more important to be happy than to follow some thousand-year-old law about not eating meat? Or not wanting the cute new boots Miri showed up wearing yesterday?

Or not liking girls.

Or having . . . you know.

I thought that you, of all people, would understand.

Maybe you've changed, though.

That's why I can't tell you what happened tonight yet.

I want to tell you. I want to tell *someone*.

I'm scared, though. It's scary to write down what happened. That makes it real. That makes it something I can't hide inside anymore. Something people will *know*.

I can't let it out yet. This secret is like a little bird peeking out of its nest, not quite ready to fly. There are scary things out there in the world.

Predators.

Storms.

Worse.

I need to build up my strength first.

Either that or hide away forever.

Love,

Evie

P.S. I miss you.

Dear Cilla,

We kissed!

KISSED.

Like "Evie and June sitting in a tree K-I-S-S-I-N-G."

Like "lips touching, me tasting her strawberry lip gloss, her probably thinking my breath smells like hot dogs" kissed.

I can't believe my first kiss was with a girl. When I was little, I used to sit on your bed while you looked through magazines and talked about the actors you thought were "sooooo cute." I agreed with you because I wanted you to think I was grown-up like you. I didn't *really* think they were cute, but I assumed I would someday.

Because that's what happens. There are steps to follow:

1. You grow up.
2. You think boys are cute.
3. You kiss boys.
4. You marry boys.
5. You have kids.
6. Your kids do the same thing.

I know the Bible doesn't say anything about girls liking girls, but what if I *do* like them?

What if I decide to change step two? What happens to the

rest of the timeline? I know I *can* marry girls, but Mom and Dad won't want me to. They'll hate me like they hate you.

(Not that June and I are going to get married. That's ridiculous. We're kids. They don't make wedding dresses that small.)

I don't know what to do, and I can't talk to Katie and Maggie about the kiss. If I kissed Joey Witter, that would be different. They'd shriek and scream and gush about how cuuuuuute his eyes are. (Which they're not. They're boring blue eyes that don't ever sparkle. June's eyes always sparkle. They're big and deep and brown, with little flecks of gold like reflected sunlight.)

If I told Katie and Maggie I'd kissed a girl, they'd give me weird looks. Or they'd tell their parents. Who'd tell *our* parents. Who'd kill me.

You're the only one I can talk to.

You know how on TV shows, first kisses are always a surprise? Like the boy and the girl bump into each other and look at each other and then all of a sudden there's kissing? Or they're watching a movie and the boy puts his arm around the girl all casual-like and then leans over to kiss her?

They never talk about what's *going* to happen; they just do it. Then there are lips and spit and moving heads and arms all over the place.

It was different with me and June. Maybe that's what I should have expected. Because we're different. We're not a boy and a girl. We're *girls*. Two girls. We're *already* different.

So we talked first. We talked a lot, actually.

We both got to the theater early on opening night. I thought Mrs. Harper said to get there at three o'clock, and I told June the same thing. She really said four, though, so we hung around outside the stage door by the picnic tables and the weeping willow tree. It was windy, so I kept pushing a stray piece of hair out of my eyes.

After I did that about ten times, June reached into her pocket and pulled out a clip. She clipped my hair behind my ear, then left her hand on my cheek for a second more.

It was only a second, but it felt like a year. Okay, maybe not a year. But way longer. She stared at me. I stared at her. I didn't know what she was thinking. I knew what *I* was thinking, but I also *didn't* know what I was thinking.

I was really, really confused. Are crushes on boys this hard?

So we stared some more.

(This is when the people in TV shows and movies would have started swapping spit.)

But we're different. So do you know what we did? We started laughing. *Snort* laughing. Holding our sides laughing. Hiccup laughing. A lady walking by with her dog stopped and stared at us, we were laughing so hard.

"Was last night weird to you?" June asked the question first. I was glad, because it felt like my mouth was stuffed full of cotton, or like if I said anything it'd come out in another language. "Us dancing, I mean? Did something about it feel different?"

I took a deep breath. I felt like I was in the middle of a dream. Not because it was my "dream come true" or anything, but because what was happening didn't feel real. It was like I was a ghost hovering outside of myself, watching some alternate-world Evie have a conversation with the girl she liked.

"It *was* weird. And different." I forced the words out, then wanted to take them back. But I made myself say more. I made myself tell the truth. "But I kind of liked it." I looked down at the picnic table, where someone had carved a pair of initials into the wood: AJ + EB FOREVER. I wondered who AJ and EB were. Amy and Elliot? Andrew and Elizabeth?

Amy and Elizabeth, maybe.

Amy and Elizabeth forever.

"Me, too," June said.

I traced my finger over Amy's and Elizabeth's initials for bravery. I took a deep breath and forced myself to ask the question I'd been wondering for weeks now. Months, even. "Do you like girls?" I avoided her eyes. I didn't want to see the look of shock I knew would be there if I was wrong. "Do you like me? Like *like* me?"

I've spent a lot of time wondering if I'm a sinner for liking June. I've spent a lot *more* time trying to figure out if she feels the same way, whether her comments about girls being "cute" mean anything. Wondering why our "hanging out" feels different than when I'm with Katie and Maggie.

Then June nodded. She didn't say anything, but she did nod. And I knew the answer! Yes! She liked me, too!

"Have you ever . . . you know . . . before?" June pointed between us. "Done stuff like this? Stuff like dancing." She looked down at our hands. They were at least a foot apart, but right then, a foot didn't seem that far. "Or holding hands. Or—"

"Kissing?" The word burst out like soda from a bottle that's been shaken up. When I opened my mouth, it was like I took the cap right off. *POP! FIZZ!* There was no way to hold that sticky-sweet stream back.

June shook her head.

I shook my head.

We were quiet for about a zillion more years.

"Would you ever *want* to?" she asked.

I shrugged. "Maybe."

"Yeah, maybe. I mean, me, too, maybe."

"Really?"

"Really."

"Um, okay."

More staring.

Did you and Alex stare at each other a lot? I mean, I know you used to stare into each other's eyes. I saw you doing that a lot. But that was *after* you'd kissed for the first time. Did you do it before, too? Did it feel this awkward?

Because this was *super* awkward. I didn't know what I was supposed to do and I didn't know if Mrs. Harper or Katie or Maggie or Miri or even Joey would walk up to us any minute.

So I inched forward and kissed her. I kissed June! Me, who used to run away from all the dogs in our neighborhood. Me, who had a night-light in my room until I was nine.

I felt like I deserved a medal for courage, like the Cowardly Lion gets in *The Wizard of Oz*.

The kiss only lasted for about two seconds, and I'm not sure who pulled away first. We stared at each other for another few seconds. June smiled. I smiled.

Then Mrs. Harper did walk up. Her arms were full of props, and she asked us to carry some stuff inside for her. I lost track of June then, and every time I caught her eye for the rest of the night, she looked away. She disappeared after the show, too. Which makes me think she regrets the kiss. Maybe *she* thinks we're sinners now, too. Or whatever atheists call bad people.

Maybe she's just waiting to talk to me about it in school on Monday. I hope things aren't weird between us now. Because even if she *does* regret it, I still want to be her friend.

Love,
Evie

P.S. I miss you. I miss your advice.

P.P.S. In case you're wondering, *Beauty and the Beast* was great. Maggie didn't lose her voice or forget any of her lines and everyone got a standing ovation at the end. Mom and Dad brought me flowers—twelve long-stemmed red roses. I bet they'd have given me poison ivy if they knew about me and June.

Dear Cilla,

Here's something I was thinking about last night in bed, when I was staring up at the ceiling, reliving every second of the kiss for the zillionth time. While I was making those two seconds stretch into two infinities.

Why did kissing June feel like a brave thing to do?

I'd never say that Katie's brave for kissing Ethan.

Why should it be different for what I did?

Love,
Evie

P.S. I miss you!

P.P.S. I'm nervous about seeing June in school today. I hope things aren't awkward.

Dear Cilla,

June wasn't in school today.

Love,
Evie

Dear Cilla,

Not today, either. She's avoiding me. I know it. She wants to forget what happened.

She doesn't even want to be friends anymore.

Love,
Evie

P.S. I miss you.

P.P.S. Please write back. I need your help.

Dear Cilla,

June's been absent *all week*. School feels so empty. Now that *Beauty and the Beast* is over, Katie and Maggie aren't as annoying as before, but they still talk about theater stuff *all the time*. Stuff like what the next show is going to be. If Katie should take singing lessons now, too. How it'll be "the best thing ever" for them to go with their new friends on a trip to New York City.

Or else they talk about Ethan and Dominic. (Maggie and Dominic started going out last week.)

I know more about Ethan and Dominic than I ever wanted to know. Like that Ethan's favorite vegetable is brussels sprouts. That Dominic's favorite color is dark green (not light green, not regular green, but *dark* green). That Ethan uses rose-scented shampoo that he borrows from his younger sister (I'm not supposed to tell anyone that part).

I know the same things about June, but I can't say them out loud. Katie and Maggie aren't going to care that June broke her middle finger last year and that whenever it's going to rain she feels a little pang there. They're not going to care that June always sneezes three times in a row. Not once or twice, but always three times. They're not going to care that June hates pasta *and* turkey sandwiches, and they're two of my favorite foods.

Katie and Maggie and I still laugh together, but it's not the same. It's not like when I'm with June. There's nothing else competing for my attention with June.

It's just us.

Us laughing about the pen stain on Ms. Pasquale's cheek that she doesn't notice for two hours. Us trying to make the best designs on the soles of our sneakers. Us convincing June's mom to share her super-secret recipe for cinnamon apple pie and then getting into a flour fight in the kitchen.

I miss her. As a friend and as (maybe) something more.

Love,
Evie

P.S. I miss you, too.

Dear Cilla,

I've waited all day for June to call me or come over. She'd shout "Surprise!" and tell me she really hasn't been ignoring me. She'd say everything's okay with us and that she doesn't think I'm gross and disgusting and a . . . you know.

You know, the word Mom and Dad use to describe girls who like other girls. The word they say with pursed lips, like they've sucked on a lemon.

A lesbian.

What if June gets that lemon face, too? I know I didn't do anything wrong, but I still feel guilty. Because of *church*. And because of our backward parents, who've talked about the "awfulness of same-sex marriage" enough that it's apparently brainwashed me a little bit.

That makes me feel kind of sick. Because I didn't do anything wrong. *We* didn't do anything wrong.

So now I feel guilty about feeling guilty about the kiss. AHHHHHHH!

Mom had to pick up a carton of eggs this afternoon (Dad wanted ice cream, too), so I went with her to the supermarket. I didn't tell her I only went because June's house is on the way. I looked extra hard but I couldn't see anyone moving behind the windows. Her mom's car was in the driveway, though, so I know they didn't go away.

I'm so confused. Should I call her? Or will that make her think I'm a stalker? Please write back.

Love,

Evie

P.S. I miss you.

Dear Cilla,

This morning before church, Dad was reading the *New York Times* Weddings section over breakfast. There was a feature on two guys who'd just gotten married. They wore matching dark suits and each of them had a little flower in his lapel. One wore a fancy fedora (I think that's the name of the hat with the big brim) and the other had curly black hair. One of them was holding a little baby in his arms. She wore this tiny frilly white dress and might have been around the age of your baby. Maybe. I'm not that great at telling how old babies are.

Dad slammed the paper shut as soon as he saw the picture. He didn't say anything, but I saw him squeeze his eyes closed and clench his teeth. He picked up the sports page instead, but I could tell he wasn't really reading it. The article was about golf. Dad hates golf.

That was fine with me, though. I didn't want to look at him. Because I knew why he tossed away that paper. I knew why that picture offended him.

Why I would offend him, too.

Love,
Evie

P.S. I miss you.

P.P.S. Do you get the *New York Times* at your school? Did you see the picture of the lady with the wedding dress with sparkles *all* over the skirt? That's the kind I want someday when I get married. If I get married.

Dear Cilla,

June was *finally* in school today! She told Mr. Gardner she'd had the flu. I think I believe her, but I'm not sure. She does look pale, and she does have a note from her mom. Plus, Maggie's out sick today, too. I don't feel sick, though. And since we kissed, wouldn't I have caught it? I'm not sure how kissing germs work. Shouldn't they be worse than the regular germs you get when you shake someone's hand?

When June sat next to me, I waited for her to say hi first. She looked like she was *going* to say something, but then Mr. Gardner started talking about the project we'll be working on this month.

Our new social studies unit is on Europe. Mr. Gardner usually assigns partners for group projects, but he told us we could pick this time. Of course I wanted to be partners with June, but I wasn't going to ask her first. That'd feel like asking her to be my girlfriend or something.

Joey claimed Katie (I think he was trying to make me jealous. It obviously didn't work), and everyone else paired up in seconds. I bet they all assumed I'd be with June.

Which is what ended up happening, after all. Mr. Gardner wrote our names next to each other on the board and asked all the pairs to pick a country from a list he handed out.

Then June and I had the most awkward conversation in the whole world:

JUNE: *Hey.*

ME: *Hey.*

JUNE: *Did you have a good week?*

ME: *I guess. Are you feeling better now?*

JUNE: *I think so. I was barfing all over the place. It was gross.*

ME: *Ew!*

JUNE: *I know! Mom hates throw up. I think she was more miserable than me.*

ME: *Oh.*

JUNE: *Yeah.*

ME: *So . . . how about we do Italy?*

It was like we'd just met, but worse. Because the day we'd met, we talked for fifteen minutes about how parachute day in gym class used to be the best thing ever and how it's totally unfair middle schoolers don't get to do it anymore. Today we sat there staring at each other.

June was wearing this orange shirt that made her eyes look super dark, like the sky at night. She'd dyed her pink streak orange, too, and she looked really pretty. I wanted to tell her that, maybe whisper it to her, but I totally chickened out. Someone could hear me. Or June might not want to hear it.

She caught me looking at her once and smiled, though.

My heart did a double beat. I could feel it in my chest. Maybe she *would* want to hear it.

Mr. Gardner called on us first so we actually *do* get to do Italy. I remember when you did your country report on Germany and I had to taste test that disgusting sauerkraut. Pasta and pizza are way yummier.

The report is due in three weeks. That means we have to meet after school and on the weekends to work on it.

I don't know if I'm excited or totally freaked out.

Love,
Evie

P.S. I miss you.

Dear Cilla,

June and I talked at school today. Not about what happened, though. Which is funny, considering how much we talked *before* the kiss.

We talked about how Dad is super grumpy now since he gave up coffee for Lent.

We talked about how June's DVR broke and now she can't record middle-of-the-night horror movies.

We talked about how Mr. Gardner doesn't let us have snacks in class but always sneaks bites of the protein bars he keeps in his top drawer. The gross banana ones, too.

We talked about everything except what really matters.

At least we talked.

Love,
Evie

P.S. I miss you.

Dear Cilla,

Today we talked about Pixar movies and debated two-piece versus one-piece bathing suits.

We talked about sour cream and onion chips versus Spicy Nacho Doritos.

We talked about Katie and Ethan kissing in the middle of the lunchroom and getting in trouble for it!

We didn't talk about us kissing at all.

It's kind of like how *we're* not talking about what happened. Or what's *happening*. You haven't written back in ages, and I'm starting to get worried that you're sick or brainwashed or something. Because I know the letters are *going* to Saint Augustine's.

Nothing's coming back, though.

Remember how I wrote that maybe Mom and Dad are worried I might try to track the baby down? That got me thinking.

Maybe I *can*. I can find her and then I can go get you. Maybe if you hear how she's doing, or see a picture of her, you'll find some closure. Or healing or whatever. Maybe then you'll be able to come home.

You'll *want* to come home.

Love,
Evie

P.S. I miss you.

P.P.S. The verdict was neither: we both want to buy tankinis for the pool this summer.

Dear Cilla,

Happy Holy Thursday! Ha, just kidding. I know this used to be your least favorite day of the entire year. When I was a kid I thought it was silly—going to church to get your feet washed? It was like going to the supermarket to get a new car. Or going to the beach to pick apples. The two things together made no sense, which made it kind of cool.

Now I definitely agree with you. We got a new priest last month. And by "new" I mean *ancient*. Father Edward is about a bazillion years old. His fingernails are all yellow and gnarled and his face looks like a huge white raisin.

Mom and Dad expect me to take off my shoes and let those hands pour water all over my feet? Yeah, right. I know Jesus washed the feet of his disciples to cleanse them and make them feel part of the Church *blah blahdeblah blah blah*, but that was about a million years ago. (Father Edward was probably alive back then.) I don't need to get my feet washed by some old guy in a robe.

My feet are clean. I took a shower this morning. I'm wearing socks.

Maybe I don't *want* my sins washed away, either.

Mom and Dad can if they want, because they have stuff to feel bad about. They *did* something wrong. And even if they didn't, they *always* worry about doing something wrong. Or feel bad about something they *might* have done wrong.

They must get tired.

Because I get tired thinking about how to make them happy.

I get tired pretending.

I don't get why I have to do a lot of this stuff anymore. Church is okay. I like the sermons, when the priest tells a story about how the Bible relates to life. But why can I only pray using the words *they* give me? Why can't I talk to God in my own words? Why can't I pray outside by the lake? Or in my room?

What if I want a different God than the one who'll hate me for who I like?

Love,

Evie

P.S. I miss you.

Dear Cilla,

Do you still believe in God? I think I do. Even though lots of stuff doesn't make sense, I still think He's up there.

I'm not sure if it's because that's what I've *always* believed or that's what I *really* believe, but in the end, I do believe. I feel better when I pray. Sometimes my prayers are answered and sometimes they're not, but it feels good to know there's someone looking out for me.

Especially now that you're gone.

Mom and Dad are making me pray now. That's what they think I'm doing. It's 1:06 p.m. on Good Friday and we're doing our yearly "be quiet from noon to three because that's when Jesus was hanging on the cross and we need to show him respect" thing. I don't understand how Catholics know exactly what time Jesus died. Or what time they took him down from the cross. I asked Mom, but she told me it was "the principle of the thing and we should accept the answers God gave us." Then she told me to sit on my bed and talk to God.

Mom's not here, though, so I'm writing to you instead. Right now, I'd rather be closer to you than to God. I'm actually running out of stationery, which is funny. When Aunt Megan gave me this, I didn't think I'd use more than a few sheets. But now I'll have to use regular paper to write to you. Or buy new stationery.

I'm hoping I won't have to, though. Maybe you'll show up the day after I use the last sheet. Maybe it's magic paper and you'll appear in a poof of smoke when I write on the very last line.

That has about as much of a chance of happening as my Hogwarts letter coming.

I think I *will* pray now, actually. I'll pray that Mom and Dad don't kick me out of the house when they figure out what's going on.

I'll pray that you're happy and your baby's safe and that June and I figure out what's going on between us.

I'll pray because it'll make me feel better, even if only a little bit.

Love,
Evie

P.S. I miss you.

Dear Cilla,

Happy Easter! This is the first Easter we've been apart since I was born. I wore my brand-new Easter dress to church this morning. It's knee length and pink, with blue and green flowers. I told Mom she didn't have to buy me a new dress since last year's still fits, but she insisted.

"It's a tradition, Evie! I buy you and Cil—" She stopped talking and pressed her lips together so tightly they turned white. "I buy *you* a new dress every year. It's part of the celebration."

I got excited at her slip and thought it was okay for me to ask a question. "Mom, shouldn't Cilla still be a part of our tradition? Can she come home for Easter?" I held my breath for the answer, but all Mom did was stare at me for a full minute.

"Cilla *was* part of our tradition." Mom's voice broke, like she was about to start crying again. "Not anymore."

"It's not like her school's a prison!" I was yelling by then. "We can bring her home. Or visit her. That could be fun, right?" Mom clenched her fist like a boxer's. I knew she wasn't going to hit me, but she still looked scary, like a volcano about to erupt.

"We can't see her." She whispered it, but I still heard her. That made me even angrier. Because we *could* see you, if Mom and Dad would stop being so stubborn. If you would stop being so ashamed.

You had a baby. It's not like you committed a crime.

Your school is only six hours away. It's not like you're in Australia.

(Even though I bet you'd love that. Remember that time we went to the zoo and you spent a whole hour staring at that special koala exhibit? They were the cutest things there, way cuter than the baby monkeys everyone else was looking at.)

Mom didn't back down, though. She kept saying, "We can't, we can't," like she was a robot or something. I got so freaked out that I went back to my room to listen to the *Beauty and the Beast* soundtrack. (It reminds me of June.)

Dad's taking the ham out of the oven now. Mom cooked about a billion side dishes. I'm in charge of dessert. I baked the cinnamon apple pie that June and I made last month. It didn't come out as good (and wasn't as fun to make this time), but I think it'll taste okay.

I'm going to e-mail June now to say hi. I haven't seen her since Thursday because of the holidays, but we're meeting after school tomorrow to start working on our project.

I'm excited. Nervous, too. So nervous that I just set up a separate e-mail account, since Mom knows my password and checks my regular e-mail every once in a while. (Not that I wanted her reading my e-mails *ever*, but I *definitely* don't want her reading them now.)

Love,
Evie

P.S. I miss you.

P.P.S. I just e-mailed June. She wrote back right away. In all caps. HI. EXCITED TO SEE YOU IN SCHOOL!

P.P.P.S. I have absolutely nothing cute to wear tomorrow.

Dear Cilla,

We finally talked about what happened.
    And she held my hand.
    I'm freaking out too much to write anything else.

Love,
Evie

P.S. AAHHHHHHHHHH!

Dear Cilla,

June's hands are soft, like she's never washed dishes in her life. Her nails are long and sharp and smooth. The pearl ring on her left hand was cold against my palm.

It was weird and so normal at the same time.

Holding hands was even better than a kiss.

We didn't kiss again. Which is good, because I think the kiss freaked both of us out. We're only in seventh grade. I know other people are kissing, but I don't think I'm ready yet. Especially the kind of kissing where spit gets involved.

I bet you're super curious about what happened. I remember every single detail. I bet I'll remember every single detail forever.

I went over to June's house to work on the project yesterday. I said "no way" to working at our house. I knew that the second Mom saw us together, she'd know what had happened. She'd have June arrested and ship me off to one of those "De-Gay Your Child" camps.

I didn't even tell her I was going to June's. I said I was going to Maggie's and crossed my fingers that she wouldn't call the Taylors.

We worked on the project for about two hours. Italy's a cool subject, especially since Mr. Gardner said we could choose any aspect of the country. I really wanted to do Italian cooking, but June convinced me to do art, since we had such a fun time painting the sets. We borrowed June's mom's laptop and searched for different artists (Leonardo, Michelangelo) and places (the Sistine Chapel, the Spanish Steps). I wasn't sure landmarks could be considered art, but June said it'd be okay.

We still hadn't talked about "the kiss" by then. We talked about a horror movie that had been on TV the night before (June watched it with her mom and I caught the late-night showing after Mom and Dad went to sleep) and giggled about how Mr. Barrett must have had a cherry Popsicle with his lunch because he looked like he was wearing lipstick when June stopped by his room at the end of the day. We talked about whether we wanted to do set crew in the fall or try out again (June wanted to try out; I decided that my performing days are over). She asked about you.

I must have looked all serious because June poked me in the side. I laughed. (Of *course* I laughed. I'm the most ticklish person in the entire world. You made me pee my pants that one time at Uncle Bobby's birthday party and the twins didn't stop calling me Peepee Evie for *three years*.)

Then June tickled me again. So I tickled her. Turns out she's as ticklish as I am. So she grabbed my hands and I grabbed hers and we wrestled a little standing up and then we got all close. We both stopped laughing. My cheeks turned red. June bit her lip.

"I guess we should get back to work," I said.

"Yeah." She bit her lip again. It was cute. "I'm sorry I disappeared for a while. I really was sick."

"I believe you," I said. I did. Really. But what happened was still bothering me. We hadn't talked for almost a week. "Were you avoiding me at all, though?"

June looked at the floor. She looked at the ceiling. I looked up, too. There was nothing there.

"Okay, yeah," June finally said. "But only because I was nervous. And scared. I've never done anything like *that* before. I thought I was bad at it. Or that my braces hurt you." She paused. "Or that you didn't like me."

"I didn't even feel your braces!" I said. "And *I* kissed *you*. Of course I like you."

I like you.

There were the words, right out in the open. I couldn't take them back. I didn't want to, either.

"I like you, too," June whispered.

It felt like someone had taken scissors and snipped open the knot that had been in my chest all week. Then I realized June was still holding my hand.

"I'm scared," I whispered.

"Me, too," June said.

We didn't say anything else. We didn't have to.

But you know what the most extra-cool, super-fantastic, best part of the whole afternoon was? We didn't stop holding hands after we were done talking. And we stayed in June's room for another hour! Sixty minutes of me turning library-book pages with my right hand and June taking notes with her left hand.

Sixty minutes of silly and awkward and sweaty and . . . awesome.

Love,
Evie

P.S. I miss you. I wish I could have told you this in person.

Dear Cilla,

Katie and Ethan hold hands in the hallway.

Miri and Nolan hold hands in the hallway. (Sometimes she even puts her hand in the back pocket of his jeans, which is way gross.)

I bet Maggie would hold hands in the hallway with Dominic if he went to our school.

I only get to hold June's hand when we're in her room. Or in my room. Or under the table at the library if we get the table in the back corner, behind the oversized books, where no one ever goes.

We've held hands every time we've been alone together since that first time in June's room. At first it was awkward. My hands were sweaty and so were hers, so they slipped against each other. I didn't know how close to sit when we were on the bed.

Here's what my head sounded like:

If I get too close, will she think I'm too forward? But if I'm too far away, she might think I don't like her. But I'm holding her hand so of course she knows I like her. But what if she's just holding it to humor me? Does she want to kiss me? Do I want to kiss her again? Does my breath smell gross?

That was all in the span of about ten seconds, too.

Did you think like that around Alex?

Dating (or whatever we're doing) is way too confusing!

I don't think I could hold June's hand in public. I'm too scared about what everyone else would think. What if people yell at me? Or I get in trouble? What if I get sent to the principal's office and she calls Mom and Dad?

I feel like I shouldn't care about that. I should tell people I like June.

I'm not ready to do that, though. It feels too weird still.

I don't want to be ashamed of myself, but I am a little bit.

I'm an awful person.

Love,
Evie

P.S. I miss you.

Dear Cilla,

After school today, June and I went out to get pizza. We'd both brought money for lunch and the choices were either Meat Surprise or Pasta Alfredo (which is basically ziti covered with glue). The clear choice was NONE OF THE ABOVE, so we were starving by three o'clock.

The pizza place was busy, but there was an empty booth way in the back. After we argued over what toppings to get (I like pepperoni, June likes pepper and onion—we compromised with half and half) and picked out which songs to play on the jukebox in the corner (Remember when Mom and Dad played their wedding song and danced in the corner? You were sooooo embarrassed!), I finally asked her *the question*.

Well, I *started* to ask her the question. Then I got nervous and we started talking about the book we're reading in language arts class. (It's called *Fish in a Tree*, which sounds like a ridiculous title, but it's awesome.)

Then we played a game where we made up life stories for the people sitting around us.

We pretended this tall guy with a black mustache was a French painter here to find the woman he'd met in Paris years ago.

We pretended the old lady picking up a to-go order used to be a famous Broadway actress.

Then we saw something that finally made me ask June *the question*: the "Are you my girlfriend?" question.

We saw two girls sitting at a booth together. They were holding hands. They weren't kissing or anything, but we knew. We knew we didn't have to *pretend* they were girlfriend and girlfriend.

They *were* girlfriend and girlfriend.

They looked happy, too. Happier than I've felt in a long time.

I *did* pretend then.

I pretended that other people in town besides us felt like this.

I pretended that I'd be happy someday, too.

I pretended that I wouldn't have to hide because I was a sinner.

It was nice. It made *me* happy.

That's when I asked the question. Because right then, I didn't care if I was going to Hell or that I was going to grow devil horns and a forked tail. I just wanted to keep being happy.

June said "yes" in a small, squeaky mouse voice. "I mean, I think so," she said. She reached for my hand under the table, then pulled it away when the pizza guy came with our pizza. He warned us that it was hot and walked away. My face felt as hot as the pizza.

"Sorry," she said. I told her it was okay. It's going to take us a long time to not be scared of the world.

Maybe we'll always be scared of the world.

At least June's mom doesn't care if she's gay. She told her that once, a long time ago. June's still scared, though. She says it's because she's already a minority and she's seen how her mom is treated sometimes.

She's afraid of making her life even harder.

I'm afraid of Mom and Dad.

But we like each other.

Is this worth it?

I don't know the answer yet.

So we ate our pizza. We played our game some more. We pretended the little boy who walked in with his mom had telekinesis. We pretended the girl flipping pizzas behind the counter was going to grow up to be the first woman on Mars.

We pretended *we* were on a date, too.

Love,
Evie

P.S. I miss you.

Dear Cilla,

We pretended at school today, too. We didn't hold hands and we didn't kiss (we still haven't had our second kiss), but we still pretended.

Being girlfriends isn't so much something you do. It's something you feel. It's something you think.

All through the day, I thought of my girlfriend.

It made the day different. Brighter, like even though it was raining outside, there were little rays of sunshine lighting my way. It was like the difference between seltzer and water. There were bubbles inside of me, popping and sizzling all day long.

I told June what I was doing at lunch, like I was confessing something really awful: "I'm pretending you're my girlfriend today."

June giggled. "I am, too." Then she bumped her elbow against mine before taking another bite of her sandwich.

It was a pretty great day. When I got home from school, I imagined what it might be like to tell Mom and Dad. I imagined they were the type of parents who would hug me and tell me they loved me no matter what.

I wished that for a while. Then I looked around the living room. At bloody, thorn-poked Jesus looking down from the wall. At the wilted palm from Palm Sunday that's still tucked behind the picture of the Virgin Mary. At the *four* Bibles in the bookshelf (one for everyone!).

I thought about the day Mom and Dad found out you were pregnant.

I realized that my wish was never going to come true. If I told them I liked girls, they'd think I'm worse than you. They'd hate me.

They'd send *me* away.

I felt alone for a few seconds, like I did that time I lost Mom in the mall when I was five. Even though I was little and Mom says I probably don't *really* remember it, I do. I remember my heart racing as fast as a cheetah. I remember how the air smelled like French fries and soy sauce from the food court. I remember thinking that Mom left me and was never going to come back again, that I'd have to sleep on one of the beds in Sears overnight.

Then I saw Mom, still in the checkout line where she'd been the last time I saw her. I'd forgotten what she was wearing and kept looking past her.

That's what it was like yesterday: like when all of a sudden I realized Mom had been there the whole time. That I wasn't alone anymore, doomed to a life wandering the mall.

Except instead of Mom, I saw Katie and Maggie.

I remembered what *they* were wearing.

I realized that maybe I could tell *them*.

That you're not the only one I can ask for help.

Love,

Evie

P.S. I miss you.

Dear Cilla,

After I wrote my last letter, I remembered something you said last year. You might not remember, but I do. It was the night of the homecoming dance and you had the biggest pimple ever in the middle of your forehead.

I bet you remember the pimple. It was big and red and gross and the color matched your dress perfectly. I saw it before you. I was afraid to point it out, but I didn't want someone else to do it first. Especially Alex. I was expecting you to shriek and refuse to leave the house, but you just shrugged and put on more lipstick.

"Can't change it now," you said.

"But aren't you afraid of the kids laughing at you?" I asked. "Do you need concealer?" Maggie's sister, Hannah, uses concealer a lot. She's very pimply.

You looked me right in the eyes. It was a very "big sister" thing to do. "Nah. I hate the way it feels. It's just a pimple. I'm not going to let something I can't change ruin the dance."

You were so mature. I remember thinking you looked pretty even with that bull's-eye on your face.

I keep thinking of what you said: *I'm not going to let something I can't change ruin the dance.*

Here's what I'm going to do: I'm not going to let something I can't change ruin my life.

I'm going to tell Katie and Maggie about me and June. This *is* the right decision.

And whatever happens, I'm going to be okay.

Because here's what I've finally realized: How can something that makes me so happy be a sin? God wouldn't want me to be sad. No one who really loves me would want that.

Love,

Evie

P.S. I miss you.

P.P.S. Wish me luck. I'd usually say "pray for me," but I'm not sure that's going to do any good.

Dear Cilla,

I was going to tell Katie and Maggie today, but I chickened out. I had everything all scripted, too.

My plan was simple: no stalling, no changing the subject. I knew that if I was going to do this, the only way would be to blurt it out, not even pausing for breath:

"You guys don't know this but Cilla got pregnant last year and Mom and Dad hated her so much they basically brainwashed her into going to some super-strict Catholic school and now she's being really weird in her letters and I'm so worried and I *really* need to find her because I think I'm gay and I don't know what to do."

Then I'd need to take a huge gulp of air so I wouldn't pass out.

I practiced my speech all day. I practiced it with June, before school. I practiced it in my head at lunch. The only time I didn't think about the big reveal was when June and I were presenting our Italy project. (Which turned out awesome. We made this fancy map where we highlighted towns and featured one piece of art for each place. Instead of using clip art, we made our own versions out of random things we found around town. June made a *Mona Lisa* out of leaves and berries. I made the Trevi Fountain out of rocks from Freeman Lake. I bet we'll get an A.)

And then, of course, I turned into a massive coward. We

were outside school, waiting for Maggie's mom to pick her and Katie up for voice lessons. June left us alone, so I could talk to my best friends on my own. It was the perfect time. It *should* have been the perfect time.

"So what's this big thing you need to tell us?" Maggie asked. She kept checking the time on her phone. Her case was new, white with fake diamonds around the outside.

I *hoped* they were fake diamonds. Maybe Maggie's parents had won the lottery and I didn't know because we hadn't been talking much.

I went over the script in my head once more. Then I imagined Maggie holding up her cross necklace and yelling that I was a sinner. I imagined Katie laughing and telling the whole school. I even imagined hidden microphones in the bushes that would broadcast my confession to the whole town.

So I didn't say anything. I made up some excuse about wanting them to help me plan a birthday party for June. June's birthday isn't even until August, so my story made no sense. They didn't notice, though, because a second later, Maggie's mom pulled up, yelling that they were late.

And I was all alone.

I'll try to tell them again soon.

Love,
Evie

P.S. I miss you.

Dear Cilla,

Mom and Dad are acting really weird lately. Like even weirder than normal. Mom's not cooking and watching renovation shows as much, but now she spends her time hovering around me. Like I'm a toddler and she's afraid I'm going to climb up the curtains. Or eat one of the shiny decorative rocks on the coffee table.

Dad keeps gritting his teeth every time he looks at me. *When* he looks at me, I mean.

I keep trying to convince myself I'm being hypersensitive, that I'm imagining all this because I think they're going to hate me.

Then I look over my shoulder and see Mom.

Then Dad leaves a room just as I'm going in.

And I get scared all over again.

Love,
Evie

P.S. Where are you, Cilla? I miss you.

Dear Cilla,

Telling Katie and Maggie is going to be scary. It's so much easier to tell you stuff in these letters. Because I don't have to see you. Because there's a gap between me writing the words and you reading them. In a way, it's like I'm really telling *nobody*.

Nobody doesn't judge me.

Nobody doesn't think I'm going straight to Hell for holding a girl's hand.

Nobody doesn't stop speaking to me or send me away to live in a home for lesbian middle schoolers. (Do they have those?)

Nobody doesn't give hugs, though. Or advice.

Talking to nobody is lonely.

So I'm going to tell somebody else. For real this time.

Then I'm going to go find you. Because this is getting ridiculous. I haven't seen you or heard your voice since June. That's almost a year. A year is a long time. A lot can happen in a year.

I don't want a year to turn into more.

Plus, Katie and Maggie don't know Mom and Dad like you do. And I need advice. I need to know whether I should tell them the truth.

And what's going to happen if I do.

Love,

Evie

P.S. I miss you.

Dear Cilla,

I did it! I did it! I told Katie and Maggie and they were . . . okay, I guess? They were definitely surprised. Shocked even. But then happy. (I think.)

After that first time chickening out, I e-mailed Katie and Maggie. I asked them when they were free and we decided on a date and time to meet at the park. I wrote it on my calendar in black marker, too, so there'd be no way to get scared and cancel.

Then I called June to see if she was free, since I wanted her there for moral support. Of course I'd picked the one afternoon she was busy. It was something she couldn't back out of, either—her grandma and uncle were visiting and they were all having a special lunch.

June told me to tell them without her, though. She said Katie and Maggie were my friends, and that if they judged me, they weren't true friends anyway. Which I knew, obviously, but I guess the words hadn't traveled from my head down to my heart. Fear got in the way, because thinking about a world without Katie and Maggie (even if we haven't talked much lately) is awful.

But a world without June would make me sad, too.

So we met at the park. The daffodils and crocuses were blooming and there were even a few ducks swimming around the pond. A little boy and his mother threw crusts into the water.

Do you remember when we used to do that? Mom would save the butts of the bread, and we'd shove a bunch into a paper bag to bring with us. We named the ducks, too: Freddie, Delilah, Marjorie, and Supergirl. You named the first three and I named the last one.

Supergirl was the coolest duck. She had that dark yellow spot on her in the shape of an S.

I pretended I had the courage of Supergirl when Katie and Maggie walked up. I said the exact words I'd planned, right away, so I wouldn't lose my nerve.

Katie's jaw dropped.

Maggie's eyes opened wide.

"Really?" Katie asked.

"You like girls?" Maggie asked. "Like *like* them? Like you want to kiss them?"

"So you're a lesbian?" Katie didn't say it like Mom does. Like the cook at Applebee's accidentally put mayonnaise on her hamburger. Or like Dad does. Like when it rains on a day he has an Ultimate game.

They weren't running away and screaming. That was a good sign. "I think so," I said. "I mean, I *have* kissed one."

"What?" Maggie shrieked. "You got your first kiss before me?" She shoved me on the shoulder, but not like she was mad at me. Like we were friends.

(Which we still are!)

I think I blushed, because it felt like I was sitting in front of a fireplace. "One kiss!" I said.

"Who was it?" Katie bounced up and down. Her curly ponytail swung back and forth. "This is so cool. First me and Ethan, then Maggie and Dominic, and now Evie and whoever!"

It was the best thing ever. Katie and Maggie acted like I'd just confessed to liking a boy, like everything was totally normal.

I told them about June. (Katie groaned. "Of course! It's so obvious now!")

I told them about you.

They were cool. They were awesome.

They are my best friends.

Love,

Evie

P.S. I miss you.

P.P.S. Katie and Maggie agree that I need to see you in person. We came up with a plan, too. It was like the musical hadn't happened, like we hadn't barely talked in months. It was the best.

Dear Cilla,

I stopped at the high school after school today. That was the first step of our plan. Class had been out for almost an hour, but there were still kids around. I wore my black raincoat and my darkest pair of sunglasses. I even took one of Dad's baseball hats to wear on my head. I didn't want anyone to recognize me, in case word got back to Mom and Dad. If they knew I was looking for Alex, I'd be grounded for a year. Maybe five years. I decided it'd be worth it, though, if Alex could help me figure out what's going on with you. Or if he had any idea where your baby is. (After all, she's his daughter, too.)

Maybe he'd agree to drive me to Saint Augustine's.

I knew Alex was on the baseball team last year, so I headed for the fields behind the high school. Practice was still going on, but I didn't see him anywhere.

I was dressed like a spy, with dark sunglasses and a baseball hat. I made sure the collar of my coat was up high, too. It was a silly disguise, but no one seemed to recognize me. *Plus* it made me feel super sneaky. I decided to risk breaking my cover when one of the players ran to the dugout for some water. I crooked my finger at him and he trotted over.

The boy said that Alex wasn't on the team anymore! He didn't even try out this year, which is really weird. Alex never shut up about baseball. He has a Red Sox shirt for every day of the week. Or he did. I haven't seen him at church in a while.

Anyway, Alex wasn't at school. And even though I could have gone to his house to see him, that seemed too risky. Like I was wearing one of those prisoner leg bracelet thingies that'd send a signal to Mom and Dad the second I got within a quarter mile of his house.

On to step two.

Love,
Evie

P.S. I miss you.

Dear Evie,

I mean it. Stop writing. Don't try to visit me. You need to learn to live without me.

Your sister,

Cilla

Dear Cilla,

I'm ignoring your last letter. I'm pretending I didn't even get it. Because I don't think you mean what you're writing. You want to see me, you really do. You're just hurting. And I'm going to help you. So . . . on with the plan!

Step two: Find Anna. (Or whatever her name is now. I still think of her as Anna.)

Katie agrees that you might be depressed. Maggie thinks that if you know Anna's happy, you might stop feeling awful about being a "teen mom." June says that maybe then you'll feel like your pregnancy was for "a greater good." I don't think I agree with *that*, but maybe Anna *is* happier with her new family.

Thinking that made me sad, though, so I changed the subject and we started investigating.

We looked online for adoption agencies near us. There were four nearby, three in Boston and one in Providence. I wrote their numbers down and we each made a call. Dad was working, and Mom was out food shopping. She's usually only there for an hour, so we didn't have much time.

(Plus, I didn't want her to know that June was over. Mom was really rude to June when she picked me up at school last week for my dentist appointment.)

All the agencies said the same thing: privacy, privacy,

privacy! They couldn't tell us anything, "under penalty of law." I tried to pretend I was Mom, but the adoption guy didn't buy it. My voice is way too high. Maybe I'd pass for Mom after she sucked from a helium-filled balloon, but I didn't think of that excuse in time.

Then he hung up on me. It was totally rude.

June suggested maybe you'd gone through an agency near your school. We called three more places, but they were all the same. Rude, rude, rude!

I keep picturing Anna. Or what I think Anna might look like: lots of curly brown hair, just like you. Green eyes and tons of freckles. A silly smile that will always make me laugh.

I'm not going to give up. I need to know she's okay.

Maybe then *you'll* be okay.

Love,
Evie

P.S. I miss you.

Dear Cilla,

Step three (whatever it's going to be—we haven't figured that part out yet) is going to have to wait. Because I have a date! (Picture me doing a happy dance in my room. Now picture me knocking over my desk chair and tripping over the pile of clothes on the floor. Because that totally just happened.)

I don't care, though. Because I have a date with June on Friday! My first date! (I'm not counting the times June and I hung out in my room, doing homework and holding hands. Those would have been the most boring dates ever.)

This is going to be a *real* date, a *double* date, with Katie and Ethan. At first I was mad when Katie said she'd told Ethan about us, but I guess he doesn't care, because he picked the movie we're going to, some action movie with race cars and underground tunnels. It doesn't sound great, but I don't care.

I'M GOING ON A DATE! With my girlfriend!

Every time I whisper it to myself, my insides feel the way my mouth does when I have hot chocolate with marshmallows, all warm and gooey.

Love,
Evie

P.S. I miss you.

P.P.S. Now I really wish you were here, because I have no clue what to wear on a first date.

Dear Cilla,

Mom and Dad are the worst. The worst EVER. They told me I couldn't go to the movies with June tomorrow.

Here's what happened: Mom and Dad were supposed to be at a planning meeting for Vacation Bible School tonight, but it got out early. So when they came home with Chinese food, June was still here. Whoops.

I know they don't like June. I also know that I do. And I *really* want them to change their minds. So I asked them if June could stay for dinner. I knew they'd be too polite to say no.

I was right. I just didn't think about what having June stay for dinner actually meant. That it also meant staying for *prayer*.

When we all bowed our heads, June didn't do anything. She just sat there, no bowed head, no folded hands, no anything! Mom stopped praying to ask her what was wrong.

"You don't know the words?" Mom asked.

June shook her head. "No, ma'am."

"Would you like to learn?"

"No, thank you." My heart was beating super fast by this point.

"Well, you should thank God for the bounty before you,"

Mom said in her very best "I know better than you because I'm a mom" voice.

"I don't need to thank God for this meal," June said. She sounded super polite, even though Mom and Dad were acting like she was saying all the *really* bad swear words. "I can thank *you*, though, for serving it to me."

I was mad at June for a second. Didn't she know she was going to get me in trouble? I wished she'd *pretend* to pray, just for a few seconds.

Then I realized something. Why *should* she pray? She didn't believe in God and that was okay. No one should force her to do something she doesn't believe in. June was right, too. God didn't give us this meal. The staff at Long's Kitchen made it. God didn't cook the meal, God didn't harvest the rice, God didn't grow the broccoli. People did that.

Why don't we thank people as much as we thank God? Maybe it would make the world a better place.

It's like when Mom and Dad told me to thank God for my good report card last year. God didn't work hard, I did!

Everything's starting to make total sense and no sense at the same time. I don't know what to believe anymore. Maybe believing in God is a habit I got stuck in. I didn't think about anything because I didn't think I *had* to. Mom and Dad believe, so it must be true.

Now I'm thinking. I'm challenging. June makes me do that. That's why I ~~to~~ like her.

Mom and Dad don't like her, though. Which is dumb.

Not believing in God doesn't make June evil. She doesn't have devil horns growing out of her curly hair. (If she does, they're really short devil horns.) She doesn't swear or kick kittens.

She believes something different. Just like you *did* something different.

The rest of dinner was awful. June chattered on about how she was going to visit her old friends in California for a week this summer and how she loves the gymnastics unit we're doing in gym class. Mom and Dad barely said anything and I barely ate anything.

After dinner they told me they don't want me to hang out with June anymore.

"She's a bad influence," Mom said.

When I protested that we had plans tomorrow, Mom said she doesn't care. She told me to cancel.

Too bad I'm not going to listen to them.

Love,
Evie

P.S. I miss you.

Dear Cilla,

Well, tonight started *out* as the best night of my life.

We met at Tony's Pizza before going to the movies. I told Mom that I was meeting Katie and Ethan instead. They actually believed me, too!

Either that or they didn't hear me tell them where I was going because I did it really quietly while they were busy watching TV.

(I learned that trick from you.)

Tony's was packed. Smelly, too, like sweaty sneakers and boy cologne mixed with tomato sauce. I was still hungry, though. I'd been so nervous all day that I'd barely eaten anything.

First date + lying to parents = SO MUCH ANXIETY.

I was more nervous about the date than the lying. Which was weird. I've seen June practically every day since she moved here, and I'd never felt butterflies like those dancing around in my stomach. They were mega-butterflies. Monster butterflies. Mutant butterflies.

We weren't just doing homework tonight. Tonight was supposed to be special. I'd spent an hour picking out my outfit and even straightened my hair. I stopped at the drugstore to buy a tube of lip gloss, too. It was my first time wearing lip gloss, and even though the color was a little too pink, it looked good. I looked grown-up.

June and I got our regular pizza. The pizza was good, but what was even more amazing was eating meat on a Friday without anyone making a big deal out of it. And without saying a prayer first. You know that old movie *Grease*, where the blond girl changes into a leather-jacket-wearing rebel by the end of the movie? I felt like that. Except with pepperoni instead of stiletto heels.

Katie and Ethan snuggled up on their side of the booth. June and I had regular chairs on our side, so we couldn't have snuggled up even if we'd wanted to. I was glad not to have to decide what to do. Being on a date was big enough.

I liked the little things, though. I liked brushing my hand against June's and not worrying what Katie and Ethan were going to think. I liked smiling and giggling and not feeling like I was hiding anything. Even if only three other people knew about us, that was enough. It was more than we'd ever had before.

We still had to be careful, though. Because everyone from school was there. Ian and his basketball friends were in the corner, burping the alphabet. The soccer girls were at the table in front of us, and Miri was bragging about the new "designer cleats" her dad had bought her. I don't think designer cleats are a thing.

Four soccer boys were at the booth next to us, including Joey Witter, who kept staring at me the way you look at chocolate cake. At least he wasn't drooling. No one wants to see that. They kept asking Ethan to join them, but he told them he was on a date. The other boys all cooed and hooted and made weird faces. I think Henry Stone might have stared between me and June a little too long then, but maybe I was imagining it.

I kept imagining lots of things. Like Miri staring at me and June.

Like the pizza cooks staring at me and June.

Like Ethan thinking mean things about me and June.

June had been right. Being out together *was* scary. It shouldn't have been, though. It should have been normal. We aren't monsters. Or aliens. We aren't even sinners. We're two girls who like each other.

It's not the worst thing in the world. And if Katie and Maggie accepted us right away, maybe the rest of the kids in school would, too.

Maybe I could do something brave again.

This time in public.

So I started to inch my hand closer to June's. Every nerve ending on my skin felt like it was on fire. My hand moved closer and closer. My heart beat faster and faster.

Then I saw something out of the corner of my eye. At first I thought I was still imagining things. Then I felt like I'd been electrified.

Mom and Dad had just walked into Tony's Pizza! They were staring up at the board (like they don't order the same cheese pizza all the time) and hadn't seen me yet. I yanked my hand away and dove under the table. Now Henry *was* looking at me like I was a freak.

June looked like I'd stabbed her in the heart. (Okay, maybe not *that* bad, but she did look hurt.) I felt like I'd stabbed *myself* in the heart.

I don't want to have to hide from Mom and Dad for the rest of my life. I don't even want to hide from them for the rest of middle school.

I don't want to live my life wondering when they're going to "shame" me away.

I don't want to *be* ashamed.

So I've decided that we'll skip step three of "The Plan" (we really should have come up with a fancier name) entirely. I might not have found Anna yet, but I need to see you now. Right away. We're even skipping the movie so I can get to Saint Augustine's sooner.

Maybe together we can convince Mom and Dad to accept the Morgan girls the way we are.

Love,
Evie

P.S. I'll see you soon!

P.P.S. In case you were wondering, Mom and Dad *didn't* see me. I think.

Dear Cilla,

I'm writing this from the car. It's dark and we're on a back road now, with no streetlights at all, but I borrowed Katie's phone so I can see. I know you're not going to get this letter in the mail, but I have to write down what happened.

I guess writing is how I make sense of things now. And I *really* need to make sense of what I saw.

After I finished my last letter, I went home. I had to pack, and I had to make some excuse about why I'd be away all night. Mom and Dad weren't back yet, though. There was a note on the fridge saying they'd gone to a seven o'clock movie.

I left my own note that I'd be sleeping over Maggie's. I hope they don't call to check up on me, but even if they do, we'll hopefully be long gone by then. Depending on how fast Maggie's sister drives (which, judging by how fast she's going now, is very, very fast), we should be there by morning.

I packed my stuff quickly. All I needed was a change of clothes and a pillow for the car. My toothbrush, too. I don't want my breath to smell like pepperoni and onion rings when I see you again for the first time in almost a year.

I still had an hour before Hannah said she'd be ready to drive us all, so I decided I had time for a little more investigating. The filing cabinet in Dad's office was locked, but I found the key right away, in the middle drawer of his desk. You used to keep the key to your diary in your middle drawer, too. (Fine, I'll apologize *again* for reading it.) Dad's filing cabinet was boring, though. Bills, instruction manuals for the fridge and the smoke alarm, stuff like that. Until I got to the bottom drawer.

That's where I found it, wedged in the very back of the very last folder. It was wrinkle-soft and torn on the bottom right edge, but it was still intact. A picture of a newborn baby. She had wispy brown hair and green eyes, just like you. She was beautiful, even though she kind of looked like an alien. An alien with a big bald spot, just like an old man.

There was a name written on the back of the picture, in Mom's loopy handwriting: *Amélie Evelyn*.

I remember how much you love the movie *Amélie*. I've watched it with you probably two dozen times. You have a poster of the garden gnome from that movie over your bed. Your bed here, I mean.

You named your baby after Amélie. And after me.

Mom and Dad have had this picture the entire time. Even after I asked them about the baby, they still lied to me. They told me they didn't know where she was or what she looked like. They told me they didn't want to stir up trouble.

They told me to leave things alone.

Mom and Dad are liars. Bible-ignoring, commandment-disobeying liars. Okay, maybe "Thou shalt not bear false witness against your neighbor" is only the *eighth* command-ment, but it's still pretty darn important. Especially when I'm not their neighbor, I'm their daughter! *And* the secret has to do with my niece! My flesh and blood.

What if you haven't seen this picture? What if they know more? They're hypocrites.

(And I shouldn't care what hypocrites think about who I might or might not like!)

Okay, we're stopping for food now. Katie wants some pretzels. June and Maggie want two of those convenience store cinnamon buns. We're going to get an energy drink for Hannah, too. She looks like she's about to pass out. I don't think I'll be able to eat, though. I'm too angry.

Love,
Evie

P.S. Maggie told Hannah that we'd mow the lawn for her all summer if she drove us to Saint Augustine's. I hate mowing the lawn, but it'll be worth it when I see you.

Dear Cilla,

~~You're not going to write back. You're never going to write back.~~

Dear Cilla,

You *can't* write back.

You can't hold a pen or a pencil or type on a computer.

You can't seal up your words in an envelope and press a kiss on the outside.

You can't sit in a desk chair and tap your pen against the table in that *tap tap tappity tap* rhythm you used to do that I hated.

You can't give me advice.

You can't come home.

You can't do anything.

Because you're gone.

Gone.

It hurts to write these words. Last year, when Katie's grandpa died and I went to the funeral, her grandma kept saying that her "heart hurt." Back then, I thought she meant she was having a heart attack, that she was feeling all the symptoms we learned about in health class: a tight chest, pain in your arm or jaw, indigestion.

Now I know that having your heart hurt isn't just a feeling you have in your body. Because yeah, my body does hurt. Ever since that morning at your school, I've felt like I've been punched in the stomach and run over by a truck.

At the same time.

It feels like there's a fist inside of my chest, squeezing my heart so hard that it's shriveled to the size of a raisin. But even though it's raisin-sized, the pain is the size of Mount Everest.

My body does hurt. But that's not the worst part.

There's something else that hurts, too, something I can't even describe. It's not something that's in me; it's something that's gone.

I feel hollow inside.

You know how some amputees can feel phantom pain in the limb they've lost? I read an article once about a soldier who lost his leg in Iraq. Every time it rained *for the rest of his life*, his knee hurt. He didn't even *have* a knee anymore and it still hurt!

That's what I feel like now. Like there's this huge hole that someone carved out in my stomach, and even though it's empty, everything inside of it aches.

Maybe that's where my soul was. Now that you're gone, it doesn't want to stay around anymore and is reaching up toward Heaven to be with you.

That sounds ridiculous.

Me writing this at all is ridiculous.

Love,
Evie

P.S. I miss you so much.

Dear Cilla,

This *is* ridiculous, but I had to write again. Writing is what I do now. It's the only thing I *can* do now. I can't talk to anyone. Not Katie or Maggie. Not even June. Definitely not Mom and Dad.

No one else knows what it's like to have their sister die. No one else has had a sister die in childbirth and then been lied to about it for almost nine whole months.

NINE MONTHS.

So I'm writing to you. Because you're the only thing that makes sense to me right now.

I'm not writing on stationery anymore, though, even though I do have one sheet of paper left. One single piece, mocking me with its bright colors and happy roses.

I won't use it, though. I'm using this notebook instead. My old, ripped notebook from last year with the torn black cover and half the pages ripped out. It's not pretty, but it matches how I feel inside.

Dark.

Gloomy.

Sad.

Angry.

I don't know whether I'm more sad or angry. It switches all the time. Right now I'm angry. I'm furious. Not at you, though. I'm not mad at you anymore. I was once, but that was before I found out the truth.

The truth that Mom and Dad aren't just hypocrites. They aren't just bad parents who were ashamed of their daughter for a teeny, tiny sin.

They're evil. They're liars. They're sinners.

I thought them keeping Amélie's picture from me was awful, but this is a million times worse. It's like when places have those Guess How Many Jelly Beans Are in the Jar? games and I guess something like fifty but it's really *four thousand and fifty*.

This is Jelly Bean Jar–worthy.

I will never talk to them again for the rest of my life.

Love,
Evie

P.S. Why did you have to die?

Dear Cilla,

I need to tell you what happened. I need to tell *me* what happened. Maybe then it won't feel so much like a dream.

Or a nightmare.

We got to Saint Augustine's School for Girls as the sun was rising. No one was around, so we had time to figure out where to park and what exactly to do. Because besides getting there and finding you, we didn't have much of a plan.

There was a half-eaten cinnamon bun and a bottle of water left from our pit stop in the middle of the trip. So even though I still felt sick, I ate the food. I drank the water. I needed something to do until people started to come out of their dorm rooms.

We figured that the dining hall was the safest bet. Everyone eats in the morning, right? And you never skipped breakfast. Well, except for the beginning of your pregnancy, when you were barfing all the time.

You never "skipped" breakfast. Not never "skip" breakfast.

"Skipped." Past tense. You're in the past tense now.

I hate the past tense.

But when girls started filing out of the dorms, all in matching blue-and-gold-plaid skirts and crisp white button-down shirts, you weren't there. I looked really closely, too. I looked at everyone. There were tall girls and short girls. Girls with short hair and long hair; blond, brown, black, and red hair. I didn't see your long brown curls, though.

Hannah was asleep in the front seat of the car, but Katie, Maggie, and June were as awake as I was. (I think *they'd* had energy drinks, too.) Maggie suggested trying the arts building, since you loved theater so much. Katie shot that down and I agreed. No one would be rehearsing at eight in the morning.

Then June suggested the registrar's office, which made total sense. You were a registered student. They'd have to tell me where your room was. I *am* your sister, after all.

The registrar's building was the one on the front of the brochure. The one that looks like Hogwarts, with the gray stone walls and tall turrets. I felt about two inches tall walking through the doorway, but I made sure to straighten my spine and hold my head up high, all that posture stuff Mom used to nag us about.

The stuff she'll never nag you about again.

I was afraid the office would be closed on the weekend, but there was a lady behind the desk. A nun, actually. She was as old as Grandma and smelled like oranges and mint. She wore jeans and a regular collared shirt, but still had on her black veil. Huge green eyes glared at me behind a pair of cat's-eye glasses. She was nice, though. She listened to me tell her about how I really needed to see you. She patted me on the hand when she said there was no student by your name registered there.

I described you, like maybe she was confused. Or you

were using some alias so you could *really* escape Mom and Dad's influence.

Nope. Nothing. Nada.

She had no clue who you were. I was about to set up camp on the floor (if I'd brought a sleeping bag, I would have unrolled it right then), when Katie yanked on my arm and pulled me out the door. June dragged me down the hall and Maggie pushed me out the front door. At first I protested, but then Katie said that the secretary was super old and probably senile, that she didn't know what she was talking about and we should explore the campus more.

I think I knew deep down that *Katie* didn't know what she was talking about, but I still followed them.

Down the tulip-lined path through the quad.

Around two girls playing catch.

Around the corner of a fancy brick building with ivy growing up the walls.

By the parking lot next to the girls' dormitories.

Straight into Mom and Dad.

We turned a corner and there they were, getting out of our old silver minivan with the *Choose Life* bumper sticker on the back. Mom looked like she'd just woken up. She probably had, since she always falls asleep during car rides longer than an hour.

It looked like they'd driven all night, just like we had.

I'd been holding hands with June, and I dropped hers right away. I felt guilty, but by then it'd be even more awkward to grab it again. Because Dad was hugging me so tightly I couldn't breathe. Mom was hovering like a mosquito, buzzing around and around.

I wanted to swat her away, but I wanted to know what was going on even more. I had no idea how they'd found me, but however they had, all that hugging and crying were not normal. They should be yelling at me for running away and lying.

Or for holding June's hand.

But no, they were crying. Crying so much that when Mom joined the boa constrictor–strength hug, my shoulder got soaked and snotty.

That's when they told me the truth. Well, after a lot of confusion and "um"-ing and telling my friends to go wait on a bench across the quad.

So now I know the truth: that secretary wasn't senile. You *didn't* go to Saint Augustine's. You didn't even enroll. You were all still deciding what to do when you went into labor.

Labor that started out fine, but that ended up not so fine.

Labor where the baby was "in distress."

Labor where your heartbeat dropped and the baby's heartbeat dropped.

Labor where you lost a lot of blood.

When Mom said the word "blood," I flashed to this mental image of you in a hospital gown stained red. Red like blood. Red like cherries, your favorite fruit. Red like your favorite T-shirt, the one you wore practically every week last year.

The doctors tried to save you, but they could only save Amélie. Mom held my hand while she told me this, squeezed it so tightly I had to pull away. I reached out again a second later, though. I needed something to hold on to that was a part of you, because with every word Mom said, you slipped further away.

I keep thinking of the time you fell off your bike in middle school. You were trying to do a wheelie and flew right over the handlebars. You scraped your nose and your right shoulder and both of your knees. Blood was everywhere, but Mom wiped you off and put Band-Aids all over you.

You were fine then. Your cuts healed. The only evidence left was that scar on your knee I always said looked like a shamrock.

There's no Band-Aid big enough for this.

Love,
Evie

P.S. I miss you so much it hurts.

Dear Cilla,

Mom and Dad told me more on the car ride home. Or they tried to. After a while, I stuck my earbuds in and turned the music up really loud. I found the angriest songs on my playlist, the ones with loud guitars and booming bass. The ones that pounded their way into my head.

That's what I wanted. Something else to fill up my head. Something to turn off my brain and block my ears.

It didn't work, though. Because even though my ears were filled with the screech of electric guitars and the banging of drums, I'd still heard what Mom and Dad had said when we got in the car, when I asked them how you could have died in childbirth. I mean, we don't live in the pioneer days. Don't people know how to deliver babies by now?

"She got an infection," Mom said. She sounded like she had something caught in her throat. "And the hospital near Aunt Maureen isn't the best." Whatever was in her throat got bigger, like one of those foam bath pellets that inflates in water.

Except this was inflating from her tears. They dripped down her face, some traveling a zigzag path and others going straight, like even her tears didn't know what to do in a situation like this.

"What do you mean 'isn't the best'?" I didn't realize I

was screaming until I heard my voice fill the car. "It's a hospital. It has doctors and nurses. They went to school to learn how to do that. Why didn't their teachers fail them if they're so bad at their jobs? And why did you send her to that hospital anyway? You *know* Aunt Maureen lives in the middle of nowhere!"

"Things happen," Dad said. "God had a plan." But for once, he didn't sound like he believed what he was saying. He sounded like he'd just dropped his cell phone in a puddle. "We didn't realize the hospital was so bad. We didn't think about complications—" Dad made a choking noise. Now the thing was in *his* throat. "Cilla got an infection and started bleeding. Before they knew it, things got bad. Really bad. Fast."

"That's why you rushed out of the house." The past nine months flashed before my eyes. Mom and Dad racing to pack their suitcases. Aunt Megan not answering any of my questions. Mom's tears. Dad's silence. Mom's obsessive cooking. Dad's transformation into a workaholic hermit. "You lied! You've been lying this whole time! Did Aunt Megan know about this, too? And Aunt Maureen?"

They didn't say anything, which totally meant yes.

"Was Cilla in pain?" I asked. "What did she look like?" I squeezed my eyes closed to stop myself from imagining it. But my brain was blank. Even my head was rejecting what had happened. All I saw was black emptiness.

I wonder if that's all you see now, too.

I wonder if you're in Heaven.

I wonder if there *is* a Heaven.

If there is, I hope you're there.

Mom started to answer, and that's when I shoved my ear-buds into my ears so hard they hurt.

I heard the music and the beats, the chords and the melody.

I didn't hear the lyrics, though.

All I heard were the words still floating around the car:

"Infection."

"Bleeding."

"Really fast."

I can still hear them.

Love,
Evie

Dear Cilla,

Here's what else I heard. Here's what they told me when we got home, when Dad took my earbuds away from me and they forced me to sit in the living room.

Jesus looked down at us from over the fireplace, as bloody and as broken as usual.

Like you were. Like I felt.

Do you know how Mom and Dad knew where to find me? It was because they knew I'd been writing to you at Saint Augustine's. Because the school had been mailing back everything I'd sent to you. EVERYTHING. Every question I had about God, every feeling I'd had about June, everything I'd *done* with June.

They knew everything. They'd read everything. That's how they knew where I was. Because I wasn't careful. I messed up. I left one of my letters on Dad's desk, the one where I wrote all about my date and Tony's Pizza and how I WAS GOING TO SAINT AUGUSTINE'S.

They know everything.

I wasn't embarrassed, though. I was angry. Because if you're dead, that means it was *them* writing to me. Mom and Dad were *pretending* to be you.

Which means those three letters weren't from you, after all. You never wrote back to me. There was a reason your letters were typed—and it wasn't just because you felt like using the computer. It was because Mom and Dad couldn't forge more than your signature. And looking back at the letters, they didn't even do that good of a job on that.

I wanted it to be true so badly that I probably would have overlooked anything.

Dad said they did it to spare me the pain of you dying. Mom said they did it because they were in denial, that they still felt so guilty about sending you away they needed to ignore what happened to you.

I say that's a bunch of bull.

At least they didn't confront me about June.

Small blessings.

Love,
Evie

Dear Cilla,

June's called every day for the past two weeks. She e-mailed me that she'd use a secret code so I'd know it was her. Two rings, then a hang up, then two rings again.

I didn't answer the phone calls. I didn't answer the e-mail.

I wonder if she thinks I'm breaking up with her. I wonder if I should care.

Love,
Evie

Dear Cilla,

Mom told me this morning that they'd never read my letters from when you were staying at Aunt Maureen's. Like that news flash was supposed to make what they'd done better.

Like they were all saintly now or something.

Their big revelation doesn't make things better, though. It actually makes them worse.

Because after you died, it's not like you were choosing to ignore my letters.

Before you died, you were.

Love,
Evie

P.S. Didn't you know that I was the one person who *wouldn't* judge you? You didn't have to hide from me, too.

P.P.S. I feel awful being mad at you now, but I am. I can't help it. If you had written back, maybe you would have told me something that could have saved you. Maybe you had a cold and that caused the infection. Maybe I could have convinced you to get medicine. Maybe *I* could have saved you.

Dear Cilla,

I've barely talked to Mom and Dad since they told me the truth. It's been more than two weeks, too. Two whole weeks and I haven't said more than "uh-huh" and "pass the peas." Every time they look at me all "parentlike," I look away. Every time they try to talk to me, I walk away.

I don't want them in my life if they took you out of it.

Love,
Evie

P.S. I still miss you.

FRIDAY, JUNE 21ST

Dear Cilla,

Today's the last day of school. I don't want to go. It's not because of the school part. I went back to school last week. I avoid June and Katie and Maggie in the hallways. I get to my classes early and don't talk to anyone. I don't even answer the teachers' questions. They don't get angry about it, either. I wonder if Mom and Dad told my teachers what had happened. What would they have said? Would they have actually admitted the horrible things they did? Or would they have twisted the truth around to make themselves look good? To make what they did acceptable.

It will never be acceptable. Because you'll never be here again.

I don't want to go to school because of the "you" part. You weren't here last night, for our traditional "last day of school eve" visit to the ice cream stand. You're not here now, to sign the yearbook we'll get today.

You won't be here for the lasts anymore. You won't be here for the firsts anymore.

Mom and Dad told me I *have* to go today. Mom says it's important to say good-bye and thank-you to my teachers. That they deserve that much for all their hard work.

Dad says going will give me a "sense of closure for the year."

That's when I lost it. All the words I'd been holding in

spilled out in a flood. It was worse than Noah's flood, and I didn't care who got caught up in the rush.

"Closure?" I shrieked the word so loud Mom literally put her hands over her ears. "You mean the closure you didn't give me when Cilla died?"

Dad flinched at your name.

"Why did you do it anyway?" I asked. "What good did lying do? You knew the truth would come out eventually. It had to!"

Mom squeezed her eyes shut. She looked like a little kid playing hide-and-seek, a kid who thinks that just because she shuts out the world, she can't be seen.

Maybe *they* wanted to shut out what happened to you, but that doesn't mean they should have made me shut it out, too.

Even if I want to do that same thing right now.

Love,
Evie

P.S. I miss how even in high school, you still called Cheerios "Cheer-di-ohs," like you did when you were a kid.

Dear Cilla,

I know I should call June.
  I want to call June.
  I know June will make me feel better.
  I don't want to feel better.

Love,
Evie

P.S. I want you.

Dear Cilla,

Maybe they're wrong. Mom and Dad never answered my question about what you looked like after you died. Maybe they didn't see you. Maybe they just believed what the doctor told them.

Maybe the doctor made a mistake.

Doctors are wrong all the time, right? They tell someone they're going to have a girl baby and they have a boy. They tell someone they have incurable cancer and then everyone prays and *TA-DA!* There's a miraculous recovery.

DOCTORS ARE WRONG ALL THE TIME. It's in the paper and on the news and everything.

I bet they're wrong about this, too.

You must have tricked the doctors and run away. Switched beds with another patient and stole their clothes.

Got a wig or a hat and snuck down the back stairs into a taxi.

Maybe Alex ran away, too. Maybe you guys reunited and you're searching for Amélie!

I wish I knew the truth. I wouldn't tell anyone your secret. I promise.

Love,
Evie

P.S. I miss you.

Dear Cilla,

I didn't say good-bye to June, Katie, and Maggie when Mom and Dad dragged me off. Okay, they didn't *drag* me off. They more carried me because I couldn't walk anymore.

I didn't even think about them until we were home, seven hours later, and I saw the halfway-open door to Dad's office. I remember first seeing the picture of Amélie and thinking that was the worst thing that could ever happen to me.

I remember telling my friends about the baby, and how June hugged me to make me feel better.

I remember how I dropped her hand like it was on fire when Mom and Dad saw us together.

June e-mails me about ten times a day. This morning she wrote that she *would* come over, but she's afraid that Mom and Dad hate her. She said she's afraid that *I* hate her, too.

I know I should care that she thinks that, but I don't. I hurt too much to care that I'm being an awful friend. An awful girlfriend.

Everyone wants me to talk, but telling my friends what Mom and Dad told me would make it real.

It's not real.

It can't be.

Love,
Evie

P.S. I miss how your bottom teeth were a little crooked, just like mine. And how you made me feel like it wasn't a big deal at all, that it made me special.

P.P.S. I'm writing this in my notebook, but I *am* going to mail it. Just as soon as I figure out where you are.

Dear Cilla,

I saw Alex today. I was sitting on our front lawn, staring at the rope swing Dad put up when we were kids. It was so windy that it kept swinging back and forth, back and forth.

It was hypnotic. It made me not think for a little while.

Then Alex drove by. I saw his red truck out of the corner of my eye, the one you always used to make fun of. Those pink dice were still on the rearview mirror, too. I remember when you bought them. You said you wanted to "girlify his truck" and "pretty it up." I remember you told me how Alex pretend-argued with you, but then put them up anyway. Even though they smelled like cherries.

Alex looked right at me when he drove by, and I looked away.

I guess you guys aren't together.

Love,
Evie

P.S. I miss you.

Dear Cilla,

I didn't go to church with Mom and Dad today. Again. That makes five *straight weeks* of skipping church—after never doing it before in my entire life! (Well, except when I've been really sick and barfing all over the place. Or that time we went to Maine for a weekend and the Catholic Church there was closed from flooding. But even then, Mom and Dad made us pray in our hotel room for a half hour.)

I can't go to church now, though. I can't look at everyone there. I can't be in the same room as them.

Because those people live in a different universe than me now. A different dimension, even. They think you're still alive, like I did last month. Like I faked myself into believing a few days ago.

I wanted you to still be alive. I almost convinced myself it was true, that you were living in Spain under a fake name. Consuela, maybe. You had a long wig and colored contacts. You wore flouncy, bright-colored dresses and rented a room from some elderly woman.

The details of your new glamorous life were always a little fuzzy, though. When I imagined it, I could never see your face clearly. Your apartment was cloaked in shadow and the fantasy always faded away in seconds.

I know you're not in Spain.

I think that's why I don't want to go to church. Because I'm jealous of everyone there. They don't know how lucky they are.

Love,
Evie

P.S. I miss seeing your face every day.

Dear Cilla,

Last night I was walking back to my room after brushing my teeth and heard Mom crying. That's not unusual. I still hear Mom cry a lot lately. I see her crying, too.

When a piece of mail comes with your name on it.

When I refuse to go to church.

When we eat another dinner in silence.

For some reason, I went into her room, though. She had a photo album spread open on the bed, filled with pictures of us when we were babies. My short wispy hair and your twisty curls. My cake-stained face and your chubby knees.

Mom had your baby picture out, too, the one they took in the hospital. It looked a lot like the one I saw of Amélie.

There was a baby blanket on the bed, one of the pink crocheted ones Grandma used to make. There were baby clothes: little pink puffy shorts and a pink flowered onesie. A purple ruffled bonnet and a knitted white sweater.

"These were my baby's," Mom said.

I felt like saying "duh," but for some reason I was trying to be nice. So I nodded.

"My first baby's," she said.

"You mean Cilla?" I asked.

Mom shook her head. I was confused, until she explained everything.

That's when I realized that Mom and Dad *had* done something wrong, back when they were young. They *weren't* always pure, sinless Catholics. *They* had . . . you know . . . before they were married, just like you did. *Mom* had gotten pregnant.

Then Mom lost the baby.

Mom started crying when she told me. Then she apologized for crying. "It's been twenty years. I shouldn't be crying anymore."

I told her it's okay to cry. Because I think I'll be crying about you for the rest of my life. I'm not going to feel bad about it, either.

Mom explained more about what had happened. How she'd gotten pregnant in college and had been super afraid it was going to ruin her life. How it almost had. She thought about dropping out of school, and it broke her and Dad up for a while.

"I loved the baby," Mom said. "But I hated the baby, too. Because I knew we weren't ready yet. Because I knew people would look at me like I had two heads. Because I was going to have to give up so much."

That's when she started crying again and explained that after two months, the baby's heart had stopped beating. She'd hated herself even more then. For doing something that would put her and Dad through so much pain.

She said that's why she and Dad are such "good Catholics." Because it had healed them. Because they thought the rules and the laws and the Word of God would save them from any more pain. From shame. From loss.

They thought it would save us, too.

But all they did was drive you away.

I almost wanted to tell Mom that it was okay. I almost wanted to hold her hand.

I didn't, though.

But I did stay in the room with her while she went through the rest of the baby clothes. I gave her that much.

Love,
Evie

P.S. I miss your hand-me-downs. I always felt so cool in your clothes.

Dear Cilla,

I was at the kitchen table with Mom when the phone rang with June's super-secret code. Mom sighed. She grumbled. "These hang-ups are really getting on my nerves." I was probably blushing, because she stared at me all narrow-eyed. "Do you know anything about this?"

I stammered a bit, but then told her the truth for some reason.

Stupid honesty lectures and their stupid lasting effects.

"It's June. But I don't want to talk to her right now." I couldn't look at her when I said June's name. I thought Mom was going to send me to my room. Or to church, so I could talk to Father O'Malley about "reforming."

Mom surprised me, though. She told me I should call June back. She told me I should talk to her.

She didn't say anything about all the stuff I wrote in my letters. She didn't say anything about our "relationship." (If June hasn't dumped me already for ignoring her and being the worst girlfriend ever.)

She just said it'd be a nice thing to call my friend.

Huh.

Love,
Evie

P.S. I miss hearing you talk on the phone to Alex, even when you talked in that sticky-sweet, ooey-gooey voice.

Dear Cilla,

I've been thinking about your baby a lot lately. About Amélie. Amélie Evelyn, if that's even what her new family decided to call her. She's ten months old now. She's probably just babbling, but maybe she's started to say a few words. "Ball" or "kitty." "Mama" and "Dada."

Her other Mama and Dada.

She might be taking her first steps. (I looked it up and most babies walk around a year. Some earlier. I bet your baby would walk earlier. I bet she's super smart already.)

She's probably picking up toys and stuffed animals and giving them hugs. (Or drooling all over them.) I wonder if she has a stuffed koala bear, too.

All the stuff I read said that babies can't form memories. Most don't remember things until they're older than one. And definitely not from when they were a newborn. I like to think that Amélie remembers you, though, that some part of you imprinted itself on her when she was born.

Like a birthmark, but on her heart instead of her stomach, like the one I have.

I wonder if one day, if I ever meet her, she'll recognize you in me.

Love,

Evie

P.S. I miss you. I miss Amélie, too, even if I've never met her.

SUNDAY, JULY 28TH

Dear Cilla,

Mom isn't cooking so much lately. Dad isn't staying so late at work. He joined a summer Ultimate team, too. Mom still hides in her room, but she mostly hovers around me, a mixture of apologies and awkward small talk and silly questions.

Here's what she asked me yesterday: "Don't the hydrangea bushes look pretty today?" I nodded and smiled, which she took as some sort of encouragement. She asked me about my summer reading and said she liked the color of my flip-flops.

She talked about how it was supposed to rain and asked me if I wanted to go to book club with her. (NO!) She hasn't mentioned June since last week, though. Maybe she's not changing her mind, after all.

Love,
Evie

P.S. I miss the way you fiddled with your starfish ring when you were nervous. I used to hate all that clinking and twirling, but I don't think I would anymore.

Dear Cilla,

June e-mailed me again this morning. She hasn't missed a day
yet. It used to annoy me, but now I'm glad she hasn't stopped.
Because I wrote back this time.

We met at the pool. It was hot today, just like it was last
year, the day the pool was closed and I first saw her at the park.

She wore a jade-green bathing suit and matching jade earrings. She has a neon-green streak in her hair now *and* her
braces are off. Her teeth looked shiny and super white. It made
me feel self-conscious about my crooked bottom ones.

June didn't say anything about my teeth, though. She didn't
say anything about my hair, either, which is super long now,
and really straggly. Or my bitten-down nails.

She said hi.

I said hi.

She didn't yell at me for ignoring her for ages and ages. I
apologized, though. I knew I needed to.

She didn't even ask what happened to you. She knew it
was bad news and she knew I didn't want to talk about it.

We just sat there on our towels, propped back on our el-
bows, staring at the pool together. At the other girls I used to
be so jealous of, the ones who don't have to worry about liking
a girl or being judged for it.

I wish I could go back to when worrying about what they

thought was my biggest problem. Even to when worrying about what *Mom and Dad* thought was my biggest problem.

June and I stayed until I remembered I'd forgotten sunscreen and my back started to burn. We went out for ice cream (I got a double scoop, one peppermint stick and one mint chocolate chip, as usual) and I told her everything.

"Cilla's gone," I said.

"I know." June held my hand then, and I didn't push her away.

"Mom and Dad lied to me. All this time."

"They shouldn't have," June said. She didn't call them names. She just listened.

"I miss her so much."

Then I cried. I got salty tears all over my ice cream. June's melted down her arm. But that was okay. We could get two more cones. We couldn't get this moment back.

After I'd finished crying, June waited for me to say something else. It was like we were at a fork in the road, and she was letting me decide which path to take. I decided to walk away from grief, if only for today.

I asked her about the last day of school. She told me that Nolan broke up with Miri in the middle of the cafeteria. That student council sold the yummiest strawberry cupcakes to raise money for a new sign. That Joey Witter got in trouble for bringing his pet snake into class. She imitated Mr. Barrett's face when he almost sat on it.

I laughed.

For the first time in two months, I laughed.

It felt weird, like I was speaking a foreign language.

I liked it, but I felt guilty at the same time. Like by laughing I was betraying you. Like by smiling I was telling you I didn't care that you were gone.

That's not true. I promise. I'm still sad.

Is it okay if I'm not sad all the time, though?

Love,

Evie

P.S. I still miss you.

Dear Cilla,

Tonight I watched a Red Sox game with Dad. We didn't talk much, but I cheered a few times along with him. He looked at me and smiled a few times, too.

Mom came into the room at one point with a batch of brownies. It was the first thing she'd baked in a few weeks, and at first I didn't want to eat one. I wanted to tell her that baking a whole roomful of brownies wouldn't make up for what they'd done.

Then I looked at Mom. She was biting her lip. Her hand (and the plate) were shaking.

I took a brownie.

"Yummy," I said.

Mom watched the rest of the game with us.

The Red Sox won by two.

Love,
Evie

P.S. I miss you more than I'd ever miss brownies.

Dear Cilla,

"Hate the sin, love the sinner." I heard someone say that once. I guess it's better than "hate the sin *and* the sinner," but I don't know why anyone needs to hate at all.

At dinner last night, Dad told me he didn't like me being with June. It was the first time he'd said her name since they admitted to reading my letters.

I knew all that baseball-watching bonding time was too good to be true. Because then Dad said that homosexuality was a sin.

I started to get up from the table, but he reached out for me. I backed away.

"I think loving a girl is a sin, but I don't hate you for it," Dad said. Like that made things any better. I waited for Mom to speak up, but she didn't say anything. I guess her suggestion for me to call my "friend" was the extent of her acceptance.

Mom took a bite of salmon and chewed it about a bazillion times. "We don't hate June, either. And we didn't hate Cilla. We just want to protect you both."

"Wanted," I said. "Past tense. You *wanted* to protect Cilla." It hurt me to say it, but it was worth it to see them flinch. "And you *can't* protect us. I might be under eighteen. I might legally be your property or whatever, but I'm my own person. Cilla was her own person."

Was.

"I can do what I want," I added. "Or like who I want." It didn't feel like *me* saying the words. I felt like someone else, someone proud of who she was.

Someone who wasn't ashamed of what other people thought.

I acted the way I wanted to *be*. Because maybe then, this bravery will start to feel more natural.

I acted the way I bet *you* wanted to act all along. It was hard, though. Really hard.

I'm starting to realize how hard everything was for you. And why you ran away instead of fighting.

I'm going to fight, though.

I told Mom and Dad that I didn't know what was going to happen with June, but that I liked her.

I told them about how I don't think I can ever trust them again.

I told them I wasn't sure about God.

I think I shocked them with that last one, but they didn't yell or scream or faint. They listened. They grimaced, but they did listen.

Then they started talking.

"Honey, you're young," Mom said. "You don't know anything about the future yet. Who knows how you'll feel in a few weeks. You don't have to be one of *those* people."

"I like girls. I like June," I said. "I *am* one of those people."

"Why don't you talk to Father O'Malley?" Dad asked. "He might be able to help you."

"He'll point you to some passages in the Bible," Mom said. "Important ones."

"I'm not talking to some old guy in a robe about who I like." I stomped my foot on the ground like a kindergartner, then realized that wasn't helping my case. "This is me and I'm not going to change. Either accept me or don't. But you can't send me away, too."

Mom and Dad looked like I'd slapped them in the face. Mom's already really pale, but she kind of looked like a ghost then. And not the nice kind of ghosts from Harry Potter, either. The scary kinds that haunt you.

The ones that are haunted themselves.

They told me they aren't going to send me away.

But then Dad said I'm too young to date.

And Mom said I shouldn't tell anyone about "what" I am.

I don't know if I'll be able to change them. That makes me sad.

But at least they didn't scream at me or lock me up.

Progress?

Love,
Evie

P.S. They miss you, too.

Dear Cilla,

Today's June's birthday. She's finally twelve, just like me!

I feel guilty that I'm not throwing her a big party, but when I told her that, she said she didn't want a party at all. I'm not sure if she's lying, but I'm trying to trust her. Because I'm still too sad to plan—or even go to—a huge party. It would feel like the balloons and streamers were laughing at me.

I bet I'd get mad at everyone else for having fun, too. *I* still feel guilty for having fun sometimes. I went for a bike ride with June yesterday and laughed while I was coasting down Tanglewood Hill. Then I started crying at the bottom. I pretended a fly had flown into my eye, but June totally wasn't fooled. (She still pretended she believed me.)

I bought her a cake, though, a chocolate one with vanilla frosting from the supermarket bakery. I used my own money to buy it and asked them to write HAPPY BIRTHDAY, JUNE! on it in big green letters. (To match her hair.)

The cake ended up saying HAPPY BIRTHDAY, JOHN! I bet the bakery worker was the same person who made the *Beauty and the Beast* programs.

We ate the whole thing and then watched a horror movie. It was fun.

Is that okay?

Love,
Evie

P.S. I do miss you.

Dear Cilla,

It's weird, but I keep thinking about my First Communion. I remember being so excited to wear that frilly white dress. Mom said I could get a new one, but I wanted to wear the same one you did, the one with a lacy skirt and pearls around the neckline.

I remember lining up with all the other kids in my CCD class outside the church. The trees were blossoming above us as we walked up the front steps. Then we all walked down the aisle, two by two. I had to stand next to Miri, who kept bragging about the gold cross necklace her parents had given her that morning. The whole time we were walking, I kept looking over at her and that shiny necklace. I wanted a gold cross, not the boring daffodils Dad had given me that morning.

Then I saw Mom and Dad on the right side of the church, below their favorite stained-glass window, the one with Jesus on the cross. The looks of pride on their faces made me feel better than a shiny new necklace ever could. I didn't think I could feel any happier, ever in my whole life.

Until they gave me my own cross that afternoon.

I wish things were that simple again. I miss believing that Mom and Dad are always right. I miss going to church and having it just be part of my routine. I miss knowing that God will fix everything, and that if he doesn't, he has a reason.

There was no good reason for you to die, though.

And Mom and Dad aren't always right.

I know that now, no matter how much they try to convince me otherwise.

Love,
Evie

P.S. We still have that old dress in the attic. I went up to look this morning, and it looks so small. You were so small then. So was I. It feels like forever ago.

Dear Cilla,

We looked through a bunch of photo albums tonight, ones I brought down from the attic. I used to think Mom was old-fashioned for always printing pictures off her phone, but now I'm glad for the bazillion albums that were stacked up there.

We started with me and you when we were kids, then looked at the ones when we were older: you playing on a baseball team in middle school, way after all the rest of the girls switched to softball.

You, caught in the act of popping a ginormous pink bubble-gum bubble.

You and me in front of Cinderella's Castle at Disney World, then just you, giving Mom a thumbs-up in the line for Space Mountain. (I totally chickened out, as usual.)

You after *My Fair Lady*, holding the flowers Alex gave you.

You and Alex, before the winter formal last year. I still think that purple dress is the prettiest dress I've ever seen.

That day, I thought *you* were the prettiest *person* I'd ever seen.

Mom said the same thing. "She looked so beautiful that night."

"She always looked so beautiful," Dad said.

Then the impossible happened: Mom and Dad apologized

to me. It was the first time they'd said the words since every-thing had happened.

"I'm sorry."

They cried. I cried. It wasn't the bad kind of crying, though, the kind that makes me feel like a black fog has entered my body and is poisoning me from the inside out.

It felt like someone had popped open a release valve, and all that fog was spilling out of me.

It's been more than a year since you went away. It's been almost a year since you died.

Maybe it's time for us to breathe clean air again.

Love,
Evie

P.S. We all miss you.

Dear Cilla,

I know now that you'll never get these letters. I know they'll stay in this notebook forever. I know it will hurt every time I look at them, just like it hurts every time I write them.

It hurts because you're gone. It hurts because I still don't know why you didn't write back from Aunt Maureen's. It hurts for a lot of reasons.

I'm still going to write, though. Because it makes me feel better. Because it's the only connection to you I have left.

I heard Mom and Dad praying the other night. Well, I think I heard them praying. They were murmuring the same way they do when they're saying the rosary. When I got closer, though, I realized they weren't talking to God. They were talking to you, telling you what they've been doing lately and how much they miss you.

Maybe these letters are my own form of prayer.

Maybe "I miss you" is my amen.

Love,
Evie

P.S. I miss you.

Dear Cilla,

Today was the first day of eighth grade. School this year is weird. Everyone knows about you now. They know that you got pregnant and that you died. They know Mom and Dad lied to me about it.

This means that everyone is avoiding me. Either they think I'm a total freak or that death is contagious.

The only people who talk to me now are Katie, Maggie, and June. Ethan, too, at lunch. It's a little bit lonely. (Which I know is a strange thing to say since I basically avoided *everyone* for a whole month.)

Maybe that's why Mom and Dad didn't tell anyone about you at first. About the pregnancy, I mean. Maybe they were afraid of being treated like this. Of being avoided or shunned. Of people feeling sorry for them.

Not that that's an excuse.

But maybe that's what started all of this. Shame and guilt and standards, the same icky stuff that got in the way of me and June being together. Because we *are* together now. She's my girlfriend still, even after all the awful stuff that happened.

At school, she sometimes brings me a little present. Something small, like a new pencil or a bracelet she made. Not that a bunch of beads on a string is going to fix what happened, but it shows she cares.

She got detention for me, too. When Danny Donato told me my parents were weirdos, she screamed at him until Mrs. Abbott had to literally *pull* her out of the room.

(Later on we agreed that they *are* weirdos, but it was the principle of the thing.)

We hold hands, too. Not all the time, and not in the hallways, but at lunch. Before school. At Tony's Pizza. We haven't kissed again, but that's okay. I don't think I want to right now.

Someday, though.

Because I'm okay with liking girls now.

That's who I am.

Love,
Evie

P.S. I miss you.

Dear Cilla,

Mom and Dad invited June over for dinner tonight. Mom made a big dinner, too. A fancy one, like she used to make when she and Dad had dinner parties for their friends.

She hasn't done that since you died.

It's getting easier to write about what happened now. You died. It happened. It'll never be over, but it did happen. I think we're all realizing that now.

Mom and Dad started seeing a therapist together. They're making me see one, too, and even though I protest a lot, it's not so bad. Colleen is young, maybe in her thirties, and really nice. She listens to me and doesn't get angry when I talk about religion or my feelings or . . . anything, really.

I think it's helping. It's helping Mom and Dad, too. I don't know what they're talking about with their therapist, but I heard Dad laugh the other day. They keep trying to spend time with me, which is kind of annoying, but not so bad. Especially since they've stopped bugging me about church and June. Especially since they're not making comments about what I "should" be doing.

Especially since they invited June over.

They were actually nice to her. Mom asked June questions about the musical (June's planning on trying out for *Shrek*) and we all talked about what kind of sets I would design for the show. Dad asked her about California. They looked at her weirdly a bunch of times, like she was a bank robber and they were trying to see where she'd hidden her loot, but they didn't say anything mean.

We didn't hold hands. I didn't want to push it.

But maybe one day soon we can.

Love,
Evie

P.S. I miss you.

Dear Cilla,

In chorus today, we sang a song from *My Fair Lady*. I loved seeing you in that musical. You were a better Eliza Doolittle than Audrey Hepburn was in the movie. I remember you telling me that after the cast list went up, two senior girls got mad at you because a sophomore wasn't supposed to get the lead role.

But you did.

Because you were talented.

You were nice and smart and funny, too.

Also annoying. You snored super loudly and cracked your gum and took showers that lasted way longer than the ten-minute rule. You stole Reese's Peanut Butter Cups from my Halloween candy stash and told me all my music was super cheesy.

But when Mrs. Harper passed out the sheet music to "I Could Have Danced All Night," I didn't remember the candy stealing or the freezing-cold showers. All I could see was you, dancing and spinning across the stage, dreaming of your future with Henry Higgins.

You got a standing ovation that night. The next night, too.

That's how I want to remember you: dreaming of your future, forever and ever.

Love,

Evie

P.S. But I still miss you.

Dear Cilla,

I saw Alex this afternoon. Sat next to him awhile, too. We didn't talk much, but that's okay.

It was at church, even though today's not Sunday. I still haven't gone to church with Mom and Dad on Sunday, even though they ask me to come every week. They still look disappointed when I say no, but they accept it. (I think.)

For some reason, I wanted to go today, though. Maybe it was the angel necklace I found at the bottom of my jewelry box, the one Dad got for both of us that time our whole family got the "Flu of Doom." Maybe it was because Katie and Maggie kept talking about the fun party they had at youth group last weekend. Maybe it was because I felt lonely and church used to make me feel better.

Whatever reason it was, I went to church today.

Maybe Alex was feeling lonely, too, because when I walked up to the altar (I still made the sign of the cross when I passed the crucifix. Total habit.), he was already there. He had his hands steepled and his head down. There were two candles shining brightly in front of him.

Vigil lights.

When Great-Uncle Paul died, Mom and Dad made an offering at church. When my principal's mother died, they did the same thing. Put some money in the little gold box by the altar and lit a candle. Then they prayed. They prayed for the person who died and they prayed for their spirit. They prayed for the family they left behind.

Alex was doing that for you. And for Amélie. He didn't have to tell me; I just knew.

He smiled at me. It was a small smile, but his mouth definitely turned up.

I smiled at him. Then I lit my own two candles and knelt down beside him.

We didn't say anything.

We just prayed.

It was nice. It made me feel a little better.

I'm still not sure about God. But anything that makes me feel better can't be that bad. Maybe I don't have to do religion exactly like Mom and Dad do. Maybe I can take what I want from it and leave the rest on the shelf, like I'm going food shopping and I decide that the chocolate chip cookies are way better than the M&M ones.

Or maybe I can buy the ingredients to make my own cookies.

Maybe.

Love,
Evie

P.S. Alex misses you, too. I can tell.

Dear Cilla,

Happy New Year's Eve! Okay, it's obviously not really New Year's Eve, but tonight we're pretending it is, since you weren't here to celebrate with us last year.

Since we didn't celebrate at all last year. So we're having our Summer New Year's party . . . in September. Which is a bit different, but I guess traditions can change.

Things can change.

Dad rented out the pool at the Radisson Hotel. Mom's over there now, decorating with streamers and twinkly lights and beach balls. She brought over a few paper snowflakes, too, to remind people it's supposed to be winter.

Mom and I went shopping for new bathing suits yesterday. When we were walking into our third store, we saw this pretty red two-piece in the mirror. It had a halter top and a little skirt.

"Cilla would have loved that," Mom said. She said it a little sadly, but mostly matter-of-factly.

"She would have," I agreed. Mom reached out and squeezed my hand. I didn't pull away. I squeezed back.

"Let's have fun for her tomorrow," Mom said. "Cilla loved Summer New Year's."

We're going to. June's coming, and Katie and Maggie. Hannah is coming and so are Emma and your other school friends. Dad even invited Alex when we saw him at the super-market yesterday. He walked right up to Alex and asked him. No dirty looks or anything. I thought Alex was going to faint. He whispered to me that he's not going to come, though. He said it would hurt too much without you there. That's okay. I know he'd come if he could.

Maybe someday Amélie will do something like this with her new family. *She'll* have a Summer New Year's. Or a Silly Hat Day. Or her entire family will take a road trip across the country to visit the World's Largest Santa. (That's a thing. It's in North Pole, Alaska, and weighs *nine hundred pounds*.)

It's nice to think she's out there somewhere, happy and safe and loved.

Love,
Evie

P.S. Tomorrow's one year since you went into labor. One year since you died. Mom and Dad haven't talked about the "anniversary" specifically, but I know that's why they planned this party.

P.P.S. That makes me happy and sad at the same time.

Dear Cilla,

Summer New Year's Eve was fun. We played chicken in the pool. (I got on Hannah's shoulders and June got on Maggie's dad's shoulders. June totally won, which was so not fair because Mr. Taylor is about a foot taller than Hannah. She gloated about it for the rest of the night.)

We had a water balloon fight and got in trouble with the hotel manager. (After he left, Dad burst out laughing and threw one more balloon at me. It was very "old Dad"–like and very cool.)

We ate hot dogs and hamburgers and corn on the cob and strawberries. Then we made ice cream sundaes from the *five* different flavors Mom convinced someone to stash in the staff-room refrigerator.

We even said a prayer for you before we ate. That made me feel good, but it didn't feel like enough. It felt like you deserved more than a fake Summer New Year's Eve party. You needed something real. Something just for you. Something where we talked about how you were gone, instead of dancing around what happened.

I'm sick of dancing. I'm sick of avoiding the truth.

You need an official memorial. The second I thought of it, I wondered why I hadn't before. Then I remembered it's because I've been avoiding the topic of where you are now.

Where your body is, I mean. I didn't want to think about it before, but all of a sudden I needed to know.

So I asked Mom and Dad.

As I asked them and they answered, I realized something. Something new and sad and kind of amazing. It was the first time I'd asked an honest question and they'd given me an honest answer in a long time. Maybe ever. It was the first time they'd acknowledged what had happened. It was the first time they'd used the word "died."

I didn't dance around what I really wanted and they didn't keep secrets because they were afraid of my reaction. I didn't get angry at them and they didn't get all judgy.

I didn't get all judgy, either, when they told me they'd buried you in a cemetery near Aunt Maureen's, instead of here, where I can see the grave and put flowers on it. Where I can visit you in one way, if not in the way I really want to.

They made a mistake. They didn't want to grieve then, so they made arrangements fast and tried to forget.

It means we're grieving more now, though.

Maybe I can help us grieve in a different way.

Love,
Evie

P.S. I miss you. Still. Always.

Dear Cilla,

I'm going to read this letter at your memorial today. I'm writing it on my last sheet of stationery. I thought the happy yellow and pink roses might hurt to look at, but I'm actually smiling right now.

It's Sunday. We're not at church this morning, but Father O'Malley is here. He's going to say Mass before we honor you. I'm not sure if you were still going to church when you died. I'm not sure if you even believed in God. But Mom and Dad wanted him here.

Actually, I did, too.

Mom lined the brick walkway with daisies, your favorite flower. She went to every flower shop and every supermarket in town. Every flower shop in the next town, too, until she had more than two hundred daisies. She bought a bunch of mason jars at the craft store and wrapped them with colored paper, then arranged flowers in each jar. I helped her put them out on the bricks. It looks nice, but also really homemade. I hope you don't mind. I don't think you will.

Dad bought a special box for me, the kind they use in time capsules. I filled it with your favorite things: Cuddly the koala and your old, ripped script from *My Fair Lady*. A half-empty pack of your favorite kind of gum that I found in your desk drawer and your journal, which I found in there, too. (I didn't read it at all this time!) *The Penderwicks*, your favorite book from when you were a kid. A baby blanket and your earbuds.

Amélie's picture.

I left enough room in there for what I'm going to add later (which will be now, and my letters, for those of you listening to me read this).

Dad dug a hole underneath your favorite tree, the maple tree you planted when you were in third grade. I remember when you first told me that it was "your" tree, I was so impressed. You seemed like God to me then. You'd created life. Well, you'd planted something in the ground. That was close enough when I was three years old.

Now you really *have* created life. You had a baby. You named her after me.

That's not what makes you special to me, though. You're special because you're Cilla. I could say so much about why I love you. I'm sure everyone here could, too. Mom and Dad. Emma. All your theater friends. Alex is here, too. I invited him and he said he'd come. He said he had to, that he needed closure, too.

We could list reasons that would go on forever, that would use up every piece of paper in the entire world. We could talk about the time you organized the food drive at school. The time you let Emma buy the last "cute green sweater" at the mall because she wanted it so much. The time you convinced me we should cook tacos and pretend to be mariachi singers for Mom and Dad's anniversary, since their first date was at a Mexican restaurant.

I don't need to list all the reasons, though. I don't need to write them down and bury them with you. You're not special because of "reasons." You're special because you're Cilla. I don't need to make a list to know why I love you.

Loving you is a feeling. It's the warmth that fills my chest when I think about you.

It's not just one memory; it's a million, twisting and twirling and wrapping together into something that looks like the pictures of galaxies in my science book.

That feeling will stay with me forever.

Your body is buried. These letters will be, too. I'll bundle this one up with the rest and add them to the box. They'll be my memorial to you, and this will be the place I can go to talk to you and feel your presence.

I *hope* I'll be able to feel your presence. But even if I can't, I know that the letters aren't my only link to you. Amélie is out there somewhere, which means that a part of you is, too. Maybe I'll never meet her. I'll be sad about that, but hopefully I'll be okay, too. Because it's enough to know she exists. That I have a niece and that you loved her.

Even though you were ashamed, I know that you loved

her. Just like even though you didn't answer my first set of letters, I know you loved me.

I forgive you for not writing back.

Because I learned from your mistakes. I learned to be proud of who I am. I learned that it's okay to grow and change, to like who I want and to believe what I want.

I don't really know what I believe or who I'll end up with, but I know what I want *now*. And I know that it's okay for me to want it.

Thank you for helping me get here.

I won't make valentines with you this year.

I'll still make them, though.

You won't see me go to high school.

I won't see you go to college.

I'll still go, though.

You won't see me have a baby, but maybe I will.

Maybe I'll have a family of my own, even if you'll never have that chance.

You won't have the chance to figure out what God is or isn't.

Hopefully I will.

You won't get to sing or dance or love or hate or tease me about all the annoying stuff I do.

I'll probably still do annoying stuff.

Things will change. Things *have* changed.

Things are still changing.

One thing will never change, though.
I'll always miss you.

Love,
Evie

Acknowledgments

There never would have been letters, never mind a P.S., without my incredible agent, Brianne Johnson, who fell in love with this story from the start, read an early revision *on vacation*, and encouraged me to raise the stakes until it became so much more. To Jean Feiwel and Christine Barcellona, I could not ask for more incisive, encouraging, sensitive, and brilliant editors. I could tell from the start that you were the right home for this book and your enthusiasm and care has made everything about this journey wonderful.

Thank you to the stupendously marvelous staff at Feiwel and Friends. There are so many of you who have championed, celebrated, and worked so hard on this book. I literally squealed out loud when I first saw the cover designed by Liz Dresner and drawn by Alice Willinger, and Carol Ly helped the interior look just as amazing. I have endless gratitude for Alexei Esikoff, Kim Waymer, Veronica Ambrose, Patricia McHugh, Kiffin Steurer, Val Otarod, and Erin Sui for their work through the numerous stages of bringing this book to life, and I am so lucky to have the wonderful Kelsey Marrujo and Melissa Zar behind me as my publicist and marketer.

Thank you to Taylor Templeton at Writers House, for her work during initial revisions and her suggestion that sparked a crucial plot point. More thanks to Allie Levick, for all her help.

A huge hug of gratitude to Kelly Hager, who read this book before I queried, encouraged me to keep going, and checked for any issues with representation.

Thank you to Erin Dionne for her constant encouragement and belief over the past six years. You answered my questions, counseled me on my career path, and helped with the parent/writing balance. You are truly a mentor and a friend.

To Lynda Mullaly Hunt, whose generous scholarship to the Whispering Pines Retreat came at a time when I was close to giving up. Your belief led me to revise this book. You are a shining star in the KidLit community.

Thanks to critique partner Jenn Bishop for helping me grow as a writer, to the New England chapter of SCBWI, and to the 2017 Debut Group and the Electric Eighteens. Having a group of writers to share this crazy journey with adds to the fun and lowers the anxiety.

To "Book Twitter," especially Rachel Simon, for making me feel like a "real writer" before I really considered myself to be one, and to the staff of the Chelmsford Public Library, for being such a wonderful day job while I wrote this book.

Thank you to Team Unicorn: Kristi Chadwick, Rachel Keeler, Margaret Willison, Amy Conway, Jeremy Goldstein, Anna Mickelsen, and Sara Marks. From grad school to Google Buzz to TMI Thursdays, you have always believed in and supported me.

Endless appreciation for my TSG girls: Patricia Moore, Erin Holt, Wendy Silver, Amy Derickson, Amanda Snow,

Mollie Lancaster, and Nicole Thomas. Thank you for listening at two in the afternoon or two in the morning and for being there through the parenting and life roller-coaster.

To my Sisters of the Traveling Anxiety: Kate Averett, Jena DiPinto, and Pam Styles. You girls listen to my crazy and tell me I'm a wonder. I could not get through this life without you. You are my lighthouses in the dark.

To my parents, Ann and Jack Clancy, and parents-in-law, Ann and Tom Petro-Roy, whose love, belief, encouragement, and babysitting hours helped this book get written and edited. Even before I was published, you believed in me enough to give me that time. My extended family has echoed my goal of being an author back to me for so long that I had no choice but to do just that. Thank you all.

Finally, and most importantly, thank you to my husband, Brian, and to my daughters, Ellie and Lucy. Thank you for understanding when Mommy had to go write. Thank you for saying you were proud of me when I first received my ARCs. Thank you for giving me time, never letting me give up, and always believing. You are my everything. I love you.

To those who feel like they can't reveal their true selves or question authority, I send you strength. You can love who you love and be who you are. You are wonderful.

P.S. To my readers, thank you for picking this book up and letting Evie into your hearts.